THL

GATEKEEPER'S

HOUSE

Eva Pohler

Published by Green Press

THE GATEKEEPER'S HOUSE, Copyright 2013 Eva Pohler

FIRST EDITION

Book Cover Design by Keri Knutson of Alchemy Book Covers and Design.

Library of Congress Cataloging-in-Publication has been applied for

ISBN-13: 978-0615882833
ISBN-10: 0615882838

Other Books by Eva Pohler

The Gatekeeper's Sons: The Gatekeeper's Saga, Book One

The Gatekeeper's Challenge: The Gatekeeper's Saga, Book Two

The Gatekeeper's Daughter: The Gatekeeper's Saga, Book Three

The Gatekeeper's Secret: The Gatekeeper's Saga, Book Five

The Gatekeeper's Promise: The Gatekeeper's Saga, Book Six

The Gatekeeper's Bride: A Prequel to The Gatekeeper's Saga

Hypnos: A Gatekeeper's Spin-Off, Book One

Hunting Prometheus: A Gatekeeper's Spin-Off, Book Two

Storming Olympus: A Gatekeeper's Spin-Off, Book Three

Charon's Quest: A Gatekeeper's Saga Novel

Vampire Addiction: The Vampires of Athens, Book One

Vampire Ascension: The Vampires of Athens, Book Two

Vampire Affliction: The Vampires of Athens, Book Three

The Purgatorium: The Purgatorium, Book One

Gray's Domain: The Purgatorium, Book Two

The Calibans: The Purgatorium, Book Three

The Mystery Box: A Soccer Mom's Nightmare

The Mystery Tomb: An Archaeologist's Nightmare

The Mystery Man: A College Student's Nightmare

Secrets of the Greek Revival: Mystery House #1

The Case of the Abandoned Warehouse: Mystery House #2

French Quarter Clues: Mystery House #3

Chapter One: Under Attack

Therese stood in the doorway, twirling a strand of her red hair round and round her index finger. There was only one bed in the center of Hecate's room. That could be a problem, even though Therese only slept about once a week.

"Maybe this wasn't such a good idea." Therese took a step back, knocking her quiver and bow against the cold stone wall.

"It will be fine." Hecate skipped forward and snatched up Therese's bag. "You can unpack your things in my closet." When she spun around toward the back of the room, her black and white hair fanned out around her slim shoulders.

Hecate didn't look like a witch or a hag or the dozens of other descriptions Therese had found on Google while visiting her family and friends in Colorado a month ago. She was an inch taller than Therese, and, in spite of the white streaks in her hair, she looked young, closer to Hermes's age, mid-twenties, with a delicate nose and thin lips. Therese knew Hecate was ancient—older than Than—but one thing she'd learned since becoming the goddess of animal companions was that immortal beings aged at different rates from humans and from one another.

"You aren't what I was expecting," Therese said with a smile.

"Mortals get me confused with Than's sister, Melinoe. That's probably it. Were you expecting someone more terrifying?"

Therese pulled her eyebrows together in confusion. "Do you mean Megaera?"

Hecate's face broke into a grin. "Those two are nothing alike." Then, in a somber voice, Hecate added, "I'm not surprised Than never mentioned Melinoe."

"Well that makes one of us," Therese said. How could he omit such an important detail? She'd told Than everything about herself and her family. Why wouldn't he have ever mentioned Melinoe? "Does she live down here, too?"

"She used to, until Hades banished her a few centuries ago. Now she lives on the outskirts of the Underworld in a cave on Cape Matapan."

"And that is…"

"On the southernmost tip of Greece." Hecate stepped forward. "Where are my manners? Meg will scold me later. Please come on inside. It's so nice to have company. I get lonely here when Persie moves in with Hades." Hecate slipped Therese's bag behind a wooden door, as though she wished to give Therese no opportunity to change her mind. "In the springs and summers on Mount Olympus, Persie and I share rooms with Demeter. Down here, I have a lot of time to myself."

Therese looked around the chamber for the first time, its dome ceiling high and covered with dancing shadows, cast by the light of the Phlegethon, the river of fire. A stream ran from an upper crevice down a series of rocks and pooled in a six-foot-wide basin before thinning and disappearing behind another smooth boulder.

"That's where I wash," Hecate explained. "The spring is fresh and good enough to drink."

Beside the basin and curled on a pillow was a small animal, a cute brown fur ball Therese had never seen. "Who's this?"

"Galin, my polecat. This is the time when she likes to sleep."

"I won't disturb her, then."

"My dog is awake and around here somewhere." Hecate glanced about the room. "Cubie? Where are you?"

A black Doberman pinscher with tall ears and a long tail crawled out from beneath the one big bed.

"There she is." Hecate reached over and patted the dog on the head. "Were you spying on us?"

"Absolutely," the dog answered.

Hecate laughed. "Cubie, this is Therese."

"Pleasure," the dog said.

"Likewise." Therese stroked Cubie's back, wishing Clifford had taken her seriously when she'd announced that she was moving out of Than's rooms. Instead, he'd given her an unconcerned stare as she had said *goodbye* and *I mean it this time.* "I have a dog, too. Maybe you would like to meet him."

"Is he intelligent?" Cubie asked.

"He's pretty smart." As the goddess of animal companions, Therese had met quite a lot of dogs, and she felt positive that Clifford was as smart as any of them.

"But probably not as smart as Cubie," Hecate said. "She was once the Queen of Troy."

Before Therese could ask why a former Queen of Troy was now a dog, the floor trembled beneath their feet, followed by a loud *boom.*

Therese clutched the wall as Hecate f

ell back on the bed and shouted, "Ahhh!"

"What was that?" Therese asked when the floor stabilized.

"I don't know." Hecate's voice was frantic. "I can't get a prayer through to Hades or to Persie."

Therese tried, too, but sensed no response. Blood pounded in her head as the ground began to quake again. She clutched the locket at her throat and prayed to Athena, but got no answer.

"Will these walls hold?" She glanced up at the ceiling, a host of scenarios playing through her mind. If the walls of the Underworld were to crumble, what would happen to its billions of inhabitants, including the souls of her mom and dad?

"Where are they—Hades and Persephone?" Therese asked.

Hecate winced as another *boom* sounded throughout the chamber. "Mount Olympus."

Just then, a crack ran across the ground, up the wall, and through the dome ceiling.

"It's going to collapse!" Therese shouted.

Small chunks of the ceiling fell on the bed, on the golden table by the hearth, and in the water basin, causing Galin to leap from her pillow and into Hecate's arms.

"Clifford and Jewels!" Therese cried. "They're in Than's rooms." Her stomach balled into a knot when she imagined them harmed.

"I'll go with you." Hecate set Galin down on the bed and spoke to the shivering weasel. "You and Cubie go to Demeter's winter cabin, and wait for me there. Okay?"

More rocks crumbled down the walls as a series of *booms* sounded throughout the chamber. The stream, which once ran gently down the wall, shot out, spraying in all directions.

"I'm not leaving you!" Galin returned to her mistress's arms.

"Nor I!" Cubie declared.

Soaked and trembling, the four of them rushed down the winding path along the Phlegethon, dodging the falling rocks. Cracks chased them all across the walls, and loud *booms* shuddered through the air. Therese was afraid to pray to Than, worried he'd god travel straight into danger. Even in her limited experience, she knew that if you arrived at a point occupied by solid mass, such as a large boulder, your body composition would momentarily meld with it. She'd discovered this problem when she once arrived in a brick wall. It had taken over an hour to recover, and the pain had been excruciating.

She found Clifford barking nervously by the hearth. "Come on, boy! We've got to get Stormy!"

Therese carried Jewels like a football in the crook of one arm as the group scurried down the narrow passageways toward the stables. She wondered if Than would be angry with her for not calling to him right away. He was already angry with her, and she didn't want to put another rift between them.

As they passed by the intersection of the Lethe and the Styx, deities cried out, and, although Therese and Hecate slowed down and searched the waters, they could not find the source of the cries. Cubie said she'd stay behind and keep searching.

When Therese rounded a corner, a colony of bats whirred up from a crevice below and fluttered past them, and then out climbed Tizzie, up from Tartarus with blood dripping down one arm.

"What is happening?" Tizzie demanded, her black serpentine curls covered in dust.

"We don't know," Therese replied.

"Well that's just great," Tizzie said, waving her hands. "The souls are in chaos. And if the pit ruptures, the Titans will be unleashed. Where the devil is my father?"

"Mount Olympus," Hecate said, dodging a falling rock that landed with a clack beside her.

Sensing Stormy's danger, Therese sent a prayer to Tizzie as she hustled toward the stables, explaining why she was on the run instead of god traveling to the gate.

I'll meet you at Cerberus, Therese added.

The three judges floated by her in their long robes headed in the opposite direction, toward the gate. Perhaps their demigod status kept them from god travel, she thought. Hecate was no longer behind her as Therese reached the stables with Clifford and Jewels. When she opened the wooden door, she found the walls had completely collapsed, and Stormy lay on his side crushed beneath the rubble with blood pouring from his flanks.

***

Among the weeping women and children, Than pulled the soul of the Chinese man from the limp body on the bed. As sorry as he felt for those left behind, Than's own troubles distracted him beyond measure. He tried to put the doubts out of his mind, but with no success. They appeared, against his will: *Therese had used him so she could become a god. She had never loved him as he loved her. The death of her parents, and so many after, had motivated her to find a way around her own mortality.*

He ushered the soul across the heavens and then down through the deep chasm, where hundreds of his disintegrated selves led other souls from different parts of the world. Like a great machine—the greatest conveyor belt imaginable—he swept along, an automatic cog in the wheel of life. And there below him on his raft, long pole in hand, was his fellow cog, Charon, ready to carry the souls to their judgment.

For centuries, he'd done this same work, longing for a change, and now that he'd finally found his wish, he was only more miserable.

Therese never meant to marry him. He'd been a fool.

In the weeks since she moved in, her eighteenth birthday and their wedding date had come and gone. Therese had said she wasn't ready, postponing their marriage indefinitely. When he asked her why, she had repeated, "I'm not ready."

Than was a patient god. Although disappointed, he could wait for as many years as Therese needed. But it wasn't her *spoken* objection that had his stomach in knots and his emotions unstable; it was the physical distance she put between them of late that made him shiver and regret the day he'd met her.

How could the same touch of his hands on her that had once made her smile and cling to him cause her to avert her eyes and pull away? If she once loved him, it was clear she did no longer.

Aphrodite had warned him this might happen.

As he neared Charon, he noticed Cerberus whining, and beside him stood his sister Tizzie. Then he saw a great explosion beyond the gates, and red and orange sparks flew through the sky. Rocks tumbled down the walls of the chasm, like the beginning of an avalanche. In all the centuries Than had lived in the Underworld, he'd never witnessed anything like this before.

"Charon," Than said. "What's happening?"

"I believe the Underworld is under attack," the old man replied in his husky, gravelly voice.

At that moment, Than sensed Stormy's death in the stables, and he disintegrated and dispatched where he found Therese, with Jewels clutched to her chest and Clifford barking hysterically at the crushed body that belonged to Stormy.

"What in the hell is going on?" Than asked.

"I don't know! We can't reach your parents. We've got to get out of here."

Before Than could respond, a thick black boulder loosened from the ceiling and landed squarely on Therese's head, knocking her and the tortoise to the floor. The tortoise slid across the ground, spinning on its back, and stopped several feet away, safe from harm, but Than heard the crunch and thud of Therese's body beneath the weight of the massive rock. His heart stopped beating as he held his breath and stared in shock.

"Father!" he shouted into the falling debris surrounding him. He felt like a helpless, desperate child. "Father!"

***

Hypnos lifted the saddle onto the beast and tightened the tack. He still wasn't used to the sharp smell of hay and feces, stirred about by the brushing by humans of the other beasts surrounding him. It wasn't a bad smell, really. Having spent most of his life in the Dreamworld, where sensory perceptions were dulled by a degree of separation between the mind and the body, he rather liked the pungent assault on all of his senses, not just the olfactory ones. Besides, his eyes were continually pleased by the prettiest girl he'd ever seen who was now bent over in front of him. The corners of his mouth twitched, and he fought the urge to slap her on the rump. Instead, he patted Hershey, the horse in his charge, and told him what a good boy he was, as he'd often heard the other humans say to their beasts.

Hip was grateful to the old Holt woman for taking him on as a horse handler yesterday when he'd shown up, unannounced. He'd finally won his father's permission to follow in Than's footsteps to journey to the Upperworld as a mortal in pursuit of a queen. Whether Hip would actually marry her was a different story. Hip realized that his brother had the right idea in finding a way to spend time in the Upperworld, and Hip wanted his turn. All these years of visiting girls in the Dreamworld didn't compare to the feeling of being in the physical presence of one.

Centuries ago, he'd come close to marrying one of Aphrodite's youngest Graces, Pasithea, but she overwhelmed him with her neediness, and he finally broke off their relationship. Since then, he'd been content playing with mortals in their dreams, but his brother's recent love affair, he had to admit, had made him jealous. He couldn't help but wonder what real girls were like and if they'd be as eager to put their arms around him in the Upperworld as they were in their dreams.

Hip hoped to soon have a taste of Jen's pretty lips. Maybe he'd get lucky and taste all of her.

Mrs. Holt looked at him now from behind the big stallion they called The General.

"You're as handy as your brother," Mrs. Holt said. "Too bad he couldn't come with you."

Jen stood up and brushed her mare's mane. "He's too busy with the wedding plans, I bet."

Hip couldn't stop the smile from crossing his face every time Jen looked at him through narrowed eyes. She recognized him, he was sure of it, but she was having trouble admitting to herself that she knew him from her dreams.

"I doubt that," Hip said with a shrug.

Jen whipped around to face him with her hands on her hips, her pretty mouth making a perfect "O." Then she said, "He better not make her do everything by herself. Damn your brother if he does."

This tickled Hip beyond control, and he couldn't stop himself from busting out laughing. What mortal had the gall to damn the god of death? Of course, this girl had no idea what she was saying.

10

"Language," Mrs. Holt said from the back of the barn.

Jen ignored her mother. "What's so funny?' She moved closer, her brown eyes glaring up at Hip from beneath her pretty blonde bangs and equally blond lashes. "Don't tell me you're a chauvinistic pig."

"Jen!" Mrs. Holt scolded from behind her beast. "Don't talk to Hip like that."

Jen kept her eyes blazing on Hip, but spoke to her mother. "I have the right to talk like that to anyone who laughs at me, Mama."

"My apologies," Hip said, reining in his chuckles. "But you misunderstood. Than's not busy with the wedding because, last I heard, Therese called it off."

Jen's mouth dropped open. Then, after staring incredulously at Hip for an uncomfortable amount of time, she threw her hands up in the air and presented him with a smile he hadn't earned. "Allelujah, praise the Lord! It's about time she came to her senses."

Was she praising *him*? Had he become her *lord*? Somehow he doubted it, but he was amused by how quickly Jen's demeanor changed from attack mode. She looked about to hug him. He liked being the bearer of good news.

"When's she coming home?" Jen asked him.

Hip shook his head. "I don't think she is. I, I…" He wished he'd kept his mouth shut. It wasn't his job to explain why a goddess couldn't live among her mortal friends and family.

Jen stepped between the horses and planted her feet inches from his. He wanted to reach out and touch her to see if she felt as good as she did in the Dreamworld. Her eyes narrowed and then

11

widened, and for a moment, he thought she had figured out who he was. But then she said, "Don't tell me she's going to stay in Texas."

"Why would she…" Hip stopped himself. "Maybe you should talk to her yourself." He turned his back to her and continued to brush the horse. This conversation was over. He'd never had to make explanations to mortals, and he wasn't about to start doing it now.

But Jen moved close behind him, so close, he could feel the heat from her body. He could smell her sweat and something else. Something fruity and sweet.

"I can't get a hold of her," Jen said in a desperate voice. "She hasn't returned any of my texts and calls in over a month. I don't know if she has her new email yet. She's not on Facebook anymore, or Instagram. Nothing. It's like she's disappeared off the face of the earth."

She has, he wanted to say. That's exactly what's happened. But, of course, he wouldn't.

Jen put her hand on his shoulder and he felt every part of him come to attention.

"Please," she said softly. "Please help me get in touch with her."

He turned and saw tears welling in her eyes. "I'll do what I can."

***

Jen was surprised by the sudden tenderness in the new handler's voice. It reminded her of something from a dream. She closed her eyes and shook her head.

"What?" Hip asked, his face close.

She took a step back. "I need to get back to work."

As she brushed Satellite, Jen stole glances at Hip. He'd taken her out to a movie over a year ago when his brother had introduced them, but then he'd never called her again after that. He'd said he'd never been to this part of the world, as though he were from another country. But he was from Texas. He spoke as if Texas were in a different part of the world.

Well, maybe all Texans thought that way.

Now he had the gall to show his face and ask for a job. He could have called her just to say, "Hey."

She glanced at him once more, and this time she noticed a look of worry come over his face, even horror.

"You alright?" she asked. He was freaking her out.

He turned to Jen's mother and said, "I'm sorry, Mrs. Holt, but I have to go."

"What is it?" Jen's mom asked, also noticing the obvious look of horror on their new handler's face.

"I can't explain," he said. "Something's not right. I need to go immediately. My apologies."

"Do you need a ride anywhere?" Pete asked, having just walked in from the pen and having overheard the last bit of their conversation.

"Um, no thanks," Hip said. "Thanks anyway, man."

13

Jen's mouth dropped open. This made absolutely no sense. She followed Hip from the barn and stood at the gate, where he let himself out of the pen.

"Are you coming back tomorrow?" she asked.

"I don't know. I hope so." He didn't even look at Jen, which hurt after the tenderness between them moments ago. She'd begun to forgive him. And now he was leaving?

"Will I ever see you again?" she cried out as he jogged down the gravel drive from her house to the road.

"I hope so," he repeated, but again without turning and meeting her eyes.

Overcome with a sudden feeling of dread, Jen opened the gate and followed him down the path. She watched him turn past a line of oak trees. When she rounded the corner, her throat pinched closed by the shock. He had disappeared.

She looked all around the one-mile stretch of road from her house to the Melner Cabin, where he was staying. Panting for breath and trembling, she knocked on the door of the cabin and got no answer.

"Hip? Are you there?" she called again and again, but the boy had vanished.

Chapter Two: Souls Unbound

Therese felt as though she were attempting to squirm out of a wet pair of tight blue jeans. Her body, heavy as a truck, wouldn't move, and her mind felt hazy, her surroundings dreamlike. Than's fingers curled around her shoulders, and suddenly she was light again, light as a feather, floating.

Unfortunately she could no longer recall why she was here or what she was doing. She'd been in the middle of saying something, hadn't she? "What was I saying?" she now asked Than. It was on the tip of her tongue.

Than bent over a boulder and hefted it into the air. "It's going to be okay."

"What is?"

She looked down and saw her mangled body in a bloody heap. Jewels hid in her slightly cracked shell a few feet away. Stormy was as crushed as she. And Clifford incessantly barked in terror.

"I'm dead?" Therese asked.

No sooner had she asked the question than a shower of rocks pummeled Than and Clifford, and the force thrust her up into the air. She reached out her hand toward Than and the collapsing caverns below her but could not stop herself from floating away. Gravity no longer had an effect on her, and nothing was holding her down. She was like an astronaut who had fallen from her spacecraft, spinning in slow circles as she hovered among the clouds.

She felt as though she were on the scariest amusement park ride ever invented and was now tumbling out of her seat. She screamed in terror, reaching out her hands to grab onto anything solid within reach. She was dizzy, frightened, and…confused.

Her mind became muddled and she found herself struggling to recall what had just happened. Panic built up in her airy chest as she grasped to remember her own name. She nervously snapped her ethereal fingers again and again, trying to remember anything about herself, but came up with nothing. After an indefinite amount of time passed, she found herself floating among treetops in woods that seemed vaguely familiar.

Yes. She knew these woods.

She grabbed the branch of an elm tree and used it as leverage to lower herself to the ground. Once her feet were on the path, she found she could keep herself grounded most of the time. Every so often she'd hover a few inches up in the air, but she managed to stay in the forest.

A familiar sound a few yards away encouraged her up the mountain, and soon she came upon what she recalled were horses and their riders. Two of the riders looked familiar, so she inched closer to the group. Before she could get a better look, the horses lifted their front legs high in the air, made a sound of terror, and scattered in all directions.

One of the riders shouted, "Steady, Chestnut! Steady!"

The rider was a young man with blond hair cut like a bowl around his tanned face. He had broad shoulders and thick, muscular thighs. She knew she'd seen him before, but where?

16

"Jen!" he shouted. "Where are you?"

"Pete!" a girl's voice replied from somewhere in the trees. "God, what happened?"

"Something spooked the horses. Maybe a snake."

The boy named Pete neared her on the horse, scanning the grass. She knew she'd seen him before. Then it came to her, and she remembered everything. She was Therese Mills and this was Pete Holt. She was in the woods behind her house, and she was...dead.

"Therese?" Pete whispered, looking in her direction.

Therese gawked at him. "What? You can see me?"

"Therese?" Pete asked again, apparently able to see, but not hear, her.

A second horse came alongside Pete's, and Therese recognized her best friend Jen in the saddle.

"Don't tell me it's a creepy ol' snake," Jen said as her body shuddered with disgust. "This time we're killing it. Therese isn't here to stop us."

Pete drew his eyebrows together and looked from Therese to Jen and back to Therese. "Yes she is. She's right there."

Jen gazed past Therese and then frowned. "That's not funny. You know I'm worried about her and dying to see her. Kill the snake, or whatever spooked the horses, while I round up the others."

Jen rode off, but Pete continued to stare at Therese. "I must be imagining things," he muttered. "Maybe I miss her more than I thought." With that, he took up the reins and trotted off.

"Wait!" Therese was left alone and frustrated, wondering why Pete could see her when Jen could not. She turned toward her Colorado house as she prayed to Than. *What's going on? Why aren't you with me?*

She stepped up on the wooden deck at the back of her house and peered through the kitchen window. Carol stood at the sink talking out loud, her red hair pulled up in a ponytail.

"Yes, you like grapes, Lynn. I know you do. Let me finish cutting them in half for you."

Two-year-old Lynn sat in her highchair. Wisps of Lynn's red hair and patches of her caramel complexion were covered with what looked like mashed potatoes. She held one hand out toward Carol and said, "I like gapes," over and over. "I like gapes." Therese smiled and resisted the urge to rush inside and kiss her little sister.

The memory of how Carol had nearly lost Lynn while she had been pregnant brought a wave of grief over Therese. If Therese hadn't succeeded in Artemis's quest to bring back Callisto, who had been turned into a bear by Hera and made into a constellation by Zeus, Lynn would not be a part of their lives. She would have been one more dead soul escorted by Than to the Underworld. It was only after Therese had proved herself beneficial to the goddess of the hunt that the life of Baby Lynn—Therese's natural cousin and her sister by adoption—had been saved.

Carol turned with a handful of cut grapes and laid them on the tray of Lynn's highchair. Lynn pinched them up in her fingers one at a time and popped them into her mouth. Then Lynn met Therese's eyes, recognized her, and pointed.

"Terry!"

Carol spun around, her eyes moving past Therese without recognition, just as Jen's had earlier. As Therese processed this new information (Lynn could see her but Carol could not), two figures entered the kitchen, and neither were her Uncle Richard. Her mouth dropped open when she recognized who they were: they were the souls of her parents.

Linda and Gerry Mills sat themselves at the granite bar as they had every day since Therese could remember, before they were killed three years ago by Ares's man, McAdams. Therese's mother had been on the verge of discovering an antidote for the Mutated Anthrax C, but Ares wanted no antidote as he urged the Middle East to make war with the Western World, hoping to see the US fall. Feeling nostalgic for those days when her parents were alive, Therese entered the room without opening the door (she didn't want to frighten Carol) and approached her mother's side.

"Mom? Dad?"

They looked at her blankly.

Then her father asked, "Is there any coffee made?"

"Dad, don't you know me?" Therese asked, rushing to his side. She placed an ethereal hand on his transparent back, but could not quite feel the feathery soul beside her. "It's me. Therese."

At that moment, Lynn pointed once again at Therese and shouted, "Terry!"

Carol took a towel to Lynn's face and said, "You silly little goose. You miss your Terry? I do, too. Her last visit wasn't nearly long enough."

Therese frowned. She had really wanted to stay longer than a week. Seven days hadn't given her time to do half of what she'd planned. She and Jen had gone to the movies with Todd and Ray one night, had gone dancing at the Wildhorse Saloon when Pete's band was performing a second night, and had gone for pizza with some friends from their swim team a third, so that had left only four evenings at home with Carol, Richard, and Lynn. But her duties as the goddess of animal companions required her attention, and she had to get back to them. Of course, she couldn't explain that fact to her aunt and uncle. And as much as she'd like to rush up to throw kisses on her sister's cheeks, she didn't want to frighten her. Therese was, after all, a ghost.

Then Lynn pointed again and said, "Cowboy!"

Therese followed her sister's finger and turned to the living room. To her horror, she found the room full of souls. They were mostly cowboys and Native Americans, and they wandered around the room as though they were looking for something.

Suddenly, Lynn started to cry, probably as overwhelmed as Therese at the sight of all these strangers wandering through their house. As Carol lifted Lynn from the highchair, one of the cowboys upset a lamp in the living room, and it toppled to the wooden floor.

"What in the world?" Carol muttered.

Then Therese's father turned a page of the newspaper, and Carol noticed the paper flutter on top of the granite bar. With Lynn on her hip, she rushed to the kitchen window and closed it.

"A wind must be picking up."

Therese rushed through the crowd of ghosts toward the front screened porch and out onto the wooden deck that wrapped around the house. Her jaw dropped when she saw thousands of souls wandering the land outside. Some walked and others floated. What on earth had happened?

***

Than pushed his way through the fallen rocks and debris of what was once the Underworld and cried out for Therese, but she had vanished. His disintegrated selves struggled to cling to the souls he was supposed to be transporting to Charon's raft, but they had nowhere to go now that Hades was in ruins. He also could no longer feel the call of the newly dead. The thought of the mortals suffering on the verge of death but being unable to die filled Than with horror and rage. More alarming was the fact that many of the souls were no longer bound to the Fields of Elysium, and even some may have escaped from the pits of Erebus and Tartarus. Than could not sense where they went. He was no longer bound to them, and they were no longer bound to Hades.

Although he could not get through to his parents, his brother appeared beside him with a look of dismay.

"Who's responsible for this?" Hypnos asked, as though he would take vengeance then and there, before the souls had been retrieved.

"I don't know. Do you have any contact with our parents?"

"None."

"Then we have no choice but to go to Mount Olympus to report what's happened in person."

"What about the dead?" Hip asked. "And what about the Titans? Are they unleashed?"

"The dead, but not the Titans," Than said grimly. "At least, not yet. Our sisters are holding the pit of Tartarus as we speak. Hecate and her familiars are helping."

"What about Therese?" Hip asked as they prepared to god travel.

"Killed. Her soul left with the other dead before she could regenerate. I don't know where." Than had barely had time to register this fact. He had already disintegrated and dispatched in the hundreds to search the earth for Therese. Another one of him had gently carried her body from the ruins of the Underworld to Demeter's winter cabin. He'd taken her animals there as well.

Than and Hip left the rubble around them and materialized at the gates of Mount Olympus. After asking the seasons to let them pass, they hastened up the rainbow steps and into the court where the gods of Olympus were convening.

Hades immediately heard and responded to Than's prayers as Than and his brother entered the room.

"Someone's put a block around our court!" Hades bellowed. He looked at his fellow gods. "Who's responsible for this destruction? Who would dare destroy my kingdom and upset the balance among the living and the dead?"

Than had never seen his father so upset before the other gods. His face had turned a hue of purple and his voice shook the court.

"Thanatos," Zeus said. "Come forward and report to us what has happened."

Than moved to the center of the ring and described the attack on his father's domain. "The dying cannot die. Those already dead are no longer bound, and the Titans will be next."

Zeus's eyes widened. "The Titans? That can't be."

"The Furies are holding them for the moment," Than added. He clenched his fists, waiting for the king of the gods to react to this bad news.

Zeus jumped to his feet. "This must be our top priority. We must all stop everything and put ourselves in the service of Hades."

Than sighed with relief and unclenched his fists and was rather surprised at Zeus's response.

"That's impossible," Poseidon objected, his sun-bleached beard framing a frown. "You know my duties consume me."

Than could relate to that, and for a moment he felt sorry for those gods without the power of disintegration.

Zeus turned to the god of the sea. "Yes. What you say is true. You alone will be excused, brother."

"But I've got several wars to mind." Ares raked a hand through his bright red hair. "I don't have time to clean up my uncle's mess."

Hades bolted across the marble floor toward Ares with a look of rage on his face, but Zeus beat Hades to Ares's side. The two brothers stood with their faces close to the god of war.

"You will serve Hades now," Zeus commanded. "Am I understood?"

Than blanched at the public reprimand Zeus gave to Ares.

Ares did not reply but gave a subtle nod before glaring across the room at Than.

Than suspected the god of war was behind the attack on his father's kingdom, but, without proof, he would not speak his thoughts. What a brazen move, though, even for the son of Zeus.

***

Jen could not get the horses to settle after she and Pete herded them back to the pen. Her mother had had to reimburse the trail riders, because the horses had seemed to lose their minds. And they had been the last trail riders of the season, since Autumn had officially arrived. Even now, with her younger brother Bobby's sweet talk, she and her brothers had a hard time removing the tack and turning the horses out. Jen used this opportunity to remind her mother why attending an online university from home was better for Jen. The family ranch needed her.

To make matters worse, Pete was freaking out.

"What's the matter with you?" their mother hollered at Pete when he had flinched, pale faced, for the millionth time. "You feeling alright?"

"No," he said. "I'm having some kind of bizarre hallucination or somethin'. What was in that stew you fed us?"

"Same stuff is always in my stew," Jen's mom replied.

Once they had turned the last horse out, Jen overheard her mother sidle up next to Pete and ask softly, "You ain't been drinking, have you?"

Pete's eyes widened into a look of reproach. "How can you even ask that? God, Mom! You think I wanna turn out like Daddy?"

Mrs. Holt dropped her head. "No, son, but some people can't seem to help themselves. I hope you'll tell me if that ever happens to you."

Pete glared at their mother. "It won't ever happen to me."

They all four headed back to the house, exhausted and nervous. The horses continued to fidget and buck out in the pasture. Jen's mom took the behavior of the horses as a sign of bad weather coming and told the kids to get washed up and stay indoors. She turned on the Weather Channel and listened as she heated up the leftover stew for their supper. Pete didn't seem to mind canceling his plans to go dancing at the Wildhorse Saloon. His face had taken on a hint of green.

When Jen returned downstairs after her shower, she was mortified by reports on the news of unexplained events occurring all over the world. Pete was glued to the screen, as though searching for answers to his own strange condition, looking less ill and a bit excited.

"People are seeing ghosts," he said to Jen, as she took a seat on the couch beside him. "Not everyone can see them. That's why they can't explain all the crazy things that are happening—windows breaking, objects floating in mid-air, stuff getting moved around. It's the ghosts that are making all that stuff happen, but most just can't see it."

"Are you saying you can?" Jen asked, afraid of the answer.

Pete looked at her with his mouth open, as though he might answer, but then he turned back to the television and said nothing.

Jen wondered if the disappearance of the new horse handler earlier that day had had anything to do with the chaos around the world.

A few moments later, Pete startled Jen by jumping to his feet and saying, "Oh, no."

"What is it?" Jen asked, still not sure if Pete was running on a full battery today.

Pete turned to her and said, "We need to get a hold of Therese."

"What? Why? I don't have her new number and she doesn't answer her cell."

Pete grabbed his hat and went to the door and pulled on his boots. "Hip's gotta know where she is. I'm driving over to the Melner Cabin to talk to him. Coming with me?"

***

Hypnos appeared beside Athena among the rubble and debris that had once been his father's kingdom. Apollo, with his quiver full of silver arrows, and Hermes with his winged shoes, stood on the other side of him, forming part of a ring surrounding Hades and

26

Persephone, who looked upon the destruction around them with utter shock. All of the gods and goddesses were there, save Zeus and Poseidon, whose own domains required their constant attention, and Hera, who had made some meager excuse that Zeus must have been obliged to accept because of some or another scandal. Despite the conflicts among the gods, all of them seemed to share in the grief felt by those who dwelled in the Underworld. Tears slid down Aphrodite's face, and Artemis raised her bow in sheer outrage.

"I know you all suspect me," Ares said, "but I swear before Apollo, before whom no one can lie, that I was not involved in this catastrophe. I've always strived to maintain balance between all forces, to level the playing fields for all parties, and to encourage healthy conflict. What has happened today strikes no such balance."

Hip had to admit he was surprised and impressed by the words spoken by the god of war, but if Ares hadn't been responsible, who had?

Hades raised his voice. "Everyone swear before Apollo and on the River Styx that you played no role in bringing destruction to my kingdom."

Hip swore and looked around at the others gathered as every single one of them echoed his response.

"We will get to the bottom of this," Artemis growled.

Athena lifted her spear in the air, as though she were about to second Artemis, but before she could utter a word, something zipped like a bullet directly at her, knocking her onto the rubble beneath their feet. The other gods surrounded her in a split second, ready to aid.

Hip found himself at the back of the crowd, trying to move in, when he heard Hermes shout, "Close your eyes!"

Hip clamped his eyes shut but prayed to Hermes. *What's happening?*

Aloud, Hermes said, "It's Medusa. She's claimed her head from Athena's shield. Athena has turned to stone."

"Athena?" Hip cried.

I'm trapped! Came Athena's silent response.

As am I. Hestia and Persephone's prayers joined Athena's in Hip's head.

Hip could hear the hissing of Medusa's head of snakes close by as he felt along the backs of the other gods toward Hermes. *Mother?*

Help me, Hypnos.

"I pierced the Gorgon with my arrows," Apollo said. "But she will not die."

Medusa laughed a shrill and rueful shriek. "Sticks and stones might break my bones, but they will never kill me!"

"My arrow struck between the monster's eyes and hangs there, impotent," Artemis said. "I see the reflection in my shield."

"My sword is useless against her as well," came Ares.

"*None* can die," Than said. "Not until the power that binds the souls to me and to the Underworld is restored."

This reminded Hip of another time in his ancient history when Sisyphus took Than prisoner, back before Hades had given them the ability to transfer one another's duties. No one could die then, either.

"I will destroy whoever is responsible for this!" Hades roared.

The ground beneath them shuddered, and something knocked Hip to the ground.

"You can open your eyes," Hephaestus said. "I've encased Medusa in a locker of solid gold."

Hip surveyed the scene. Athena had turned to white stone, with her spear raised and her mouth wide open, her knees bent. He could hear her prayers from inside the stone.

Beside her were Hestia and Persephone, also solid stone and crouched in defensive postures, eyes wide. Hip rushed to his mother's side where Than already stood, touching her shoulder.

Hades roared like a lion and raised his fists in the air. Then he moved to Persephone's side and cupped her smooth stone face in his hands. "I will fix this, my love. You won't remain in this state for long. I promise."

Hip could see the look on his father's face, and he hoped his mother and Hestia and Athena could not. For once, fear and vulnerability clouded Hades's usually confident exterior, which allowed Hip's own fear to magnify. He turned to see Deimos and Phobos, Panic and Fear, standing behind him beside their mother, Aphrodite.

"Please leave us," Aphrodite told her sons. "Your presence cannot help us."

The twins vanished.

Although their disappearance improved Hip's mood, another crisis thundered inside his head. Amid the prayers he heard for a good night's rest and sweet dreams were the shouts of two familiar mortal voices. Jen and her older brother were calling to him. He could see them above, pounding on the doors and windows of the log cabin near their ranch in Colorado.

Chapter Three: Restoration

Despite Lynn's unceasing cries, Therese remained with her parents, hoping for even the briefest moment of recognition. If they had found their way back to their house, surely they might also find their way back to their family.

"Your name is Gerald Mills," Therese said again. "And you are Linda. I'm your daughter, Therese. We lived here in this house. Dad, you were a writer. Mom, you were a scientist and worked at Fort Lewis College. That's your sister, Carol, over there."

"Oh," Linda said. "I remember Carol."

"You do?" Therese jumped up from the barstool. "You grew up in San Antonio."

"That's right," Linda said. "Gerry and I met in college."

"We did?" Gerry looked at her mother blankly.

"Therese?" Linda said, her face stretching into bewilderment. "I think it's finally coming back to me."

"You mean you can remember me?" Therese asked, trying not to get her hopes up.

Linda turned first to Gerry and then back to Therese. "I was shot. We drowned. Therese, are we, aren't we..."

"Mom!" Therese flung her ethereal arms around her mother's transparent neck, and although she could not feel her, Therese was overcome with joy. "Oh, Mom! I've missed you so much!"

"I want to remember, too," Gerry said. "You said I was a writer. What did I write?"

"Crime fiction," Therese replied. *The Catcher's Mitt, The Silent Key…*" Therese named off a few of her father's novels.

Her father shook his head. "Why can't I remember?"

Therese racked her brain for an answer. Why could her mother remember and her father not? Then an idea hit her, and she said, "Mom's memory was sparked by Carol. Maybe you need something from your childhood."

"Did I have any brothers and sisters?" he asked.

"No, but I have picture of you and your parents up in my room. Will you follow me upstairs?"

The house was still crowded with the ghosts of many strangers wandering around, as though they were lost or looking for something to help them figure out who they were and what was happening to them. Carol sat among them in a rocking chair trying to soothe Lynn, who wailed in her mother's arms, apparently not interested in the bottle of warm milk Carol was trying to coax her into drinking.

"Hush little baby, don't say a word," Carol sang.

Therese led her parents up the stairs to her bedroom, passing by other souls on the way. Therese avoided making eye contact with any of them, hoping they wouldn't ask her questions, since she had no answers. Once she and her parents were in her room, she maneuvered through the crowd of souls gathered there and found the photo album tucked beneath her old bed. She drew it out and opened it, flipping through the pages until she found the one she was searching for.

"Here you are." She held the album out to her father and pointed to him pictured as a boy standing between his parents in front of an old barn.

"I remember!" he said. "I remember my parents. I know that barn." He turned and looked first at his wife and then at his daughter. "Linda? Therese?"

"Dad!" Therese threw her arms around her father, and though they could not feel one another's embrace, they nevertheless cried tearless sobs. "I can't believe I'm getting this chance to talk with you two again! I didn't think it would ever be possible." She put one arm around each of them, not minding that she felt no warmth, no comforting flesh. "I missed you both so much." Then a thought crossed her mind. "You aren't figments, are you?"

"What's a figment?" her mother asked.

"They're eel-like nymphs that take the forms of people and things in your dreams. Figments, I command you to show yourselves!"

The souls of her mother and father stared blankly back at her, and she sighed with relief.

***

Than watched on with a mixture of admiration and grief as his father lifted his arms and commanded the debris to retake its original form. The magnificence of the power Hades could wield was breathtaking and awe-inspiring, but Hades would need at least one day to recover from the excessive use of power. This would make the Underworld even that much more vulnerable to another attack.

At Hades's command, the rocks lifted from the ground, causing a rumbling sound to reverberate all around them. One moment, the gods were standing in the soft haze of dusk beneath a cloudless sky on a giant mountain of rubble, and the next moment, they were standing in the beautifully restored jewel-encrusted palace that belonged to Than's parents.

Than's sisters, the Furies, arrived minutes later in response to their father's summons. Hecate and her two familiars were with them.

Alecto, whose short red hair stood up like flames around her head, spoke first. "We kept all the prisoners of Tartarus secure save Medusa and one other."

Hades, weakened, sat in his chair and frowned. "Who?"

"King Sisyphus," Meg replied anxiously, averting her ice blue eyes. "I and my falcon chased after him for miles, but we've been unable to locate him. I've failed you, father."

Hades's face transformed into a smile as he put his hands on Meg's shoulders. "On the contrary. You ladies saved the day. Had anyone other than old Sisyphus escaped, we would have had another epic battle on our hands."

"We may still, Lord Hades," Apollo said.

Hades turned to face the other gods gathered around him. "Right you are, nephew, but allow me a moment to express my relief and gratitude to my hardworking daughters and to dear Hecate, who haven't yet heard the worst of it."

"Of course," Apollo said. "My apologies."

"Tell us father," Tizzie pleaded. "What's happened?"

"Mother!" Meg cried. "Look!" She pointed to the statue of Persephone crouched in stone beside Hestia and Athena.

"She's trapped in there!" Alecto moved to their mother's side. "I can hear her."

"Oh, Athena!" Meg gasped. "And dear Hestia!"

Hades explained what had happened and then instructed the Furies to assist Artemis and Apollo in discovering the culprit while Hephaestus and Hermes remained behind to help guard the Underworld from any future attacks. The latter would also check all of the entrances and make certain Cerberus, the Hydra, and the other beasts guarding them were properly restored.

"What about Ares and me?" Aphrodite asked, looking hurt. "Zeus commanded us to aid you as well."

"Believe me, dear niece, the restoration of my kingdom will require all of our efforts," Hades replied. "I need you and Ares to help my sons recover the billions of souls, which escaped the Elysian Fields, and bring them before the judges to be sentenced once again. You should also be on the lookout for Sisyphus. Who knows what mischief he will cause?"

"You don't suppose that was the purpose of this attack?" Ares asked. "Who would gain by freeing Sisyphus?"

"The Furies will investigate that angle." Then Hades added, "Hecate, I need you to stand guard over these three goddesses and make sure no further harm comes to them in their vulnerable state."

"Yes, my lord," Hecate said. "But, please sir, where is Therese?"

Hades turned to Than, who explained to the others what had happened. "I can sense those who are about to die, but I'm no longer bound to those who've already passed. In short, I can't find her."

The grim looks on their faces made him feel less, rather than more, confident that he would ever successfully reunite Therese's soul with her body and restore her as the goddess of animal companions.

***

After knocking on all the doors and windows for twenty minutes, Jen and Pete sat in rockers on the wooden deck of the Melner cabin to wait for their new handler to return.

"Tell me the truth," Jen said again. She wanted to wring her brother's neck. "I can tell something's up."

"I just got a bad feeling is all," Pete replied. "Hip will know how to get a hold of Than."

"There's more to it than that. You saw her, didn't you," Jen said without inflection. "You won't tell me, but you saw Therese's ghost. You think she's dead."

Pete looked down at his boots.

Jen covered her face with her hands. "Just tell me. I can handle it."

He was silent for several more minutes. Then he said, "Okay. I saw her."

36

Jen's face shot up. "Can you see her now?"

Pete shook his head. "It was in the woods, earlier, during the trail ride. You assumed it was a snake that spooked the horses, but it was her."

Jen narrowed her eyes. She knew Pete wasn't lying, but maybe there was something wrong with him. And yet, how could she explain all the other supposed ghost sightings and unexplainable events on the news? She thought of the crown and wondered if she should share its secret with Pete. Maybe whatever had made the crown work had also given Therese the power to be invisible, and maybe Pete had the ability to see her anyway. Maybe Therese was fine and was wandering around incognito, like Jen sometimes did. But then why couldn't Pete see Jen while she was wearing the crown?

Jen hadn't worn the crown much lately, now that her father was permanently disabled from a stroke and staying at the assisted living center in Durango. But there was a time when that crown had meant the world to her. It had saved her from running away—or from something worse. She thought of Vicki and of Vicki's mother and shivered.

The sun was beginning to set behind the mountains on the other side of the reservoir, but the pretty pinks and orange hues spread across the clouds only added to Jen's frustration. She was willing to sit on the deck of the Melner cabin all night, if that's what it took to finally get some answers.

"Please, Hip," she said in her mind. "Come back. I'll do anything."

***

Ah, hell, Hip thought as he flew alone in the evening sky in the treetops of Greece. Just when he was finally making a little progress with the mortal girl, all hell had to break loose. He'd been so close to touching her. Her face had been inches from his. He'd had the feeling Jen would have been in his bed within the week. He could hear her calling to him, prime for kissing. She was saying she'd do anything…

He held the siphon Hades and Hephaestus had constructed with a reservoir of water from the Lethe on one side and a funnel inlaid with magic crystals on the other. He'd never used one of these contraptions before, but apparently it was meant to suction up the souls, like a vacuum cleaner. Than, Aphrodite, Ares, and he had divided up the global territories and, each with a siphon, had taken up the boring, uneventful task of sucking up the dead. Weren't there lesser gods who could take this job? He had overheard Ares and Aphrodite recruiting their kids—the twins, Cupid, Harmonia, and even Anteros, who often went and undid the very love Cupid inspired. Talk about sibling rivalry. Aphrodite and Ares seemed to have made a specialty of creating children of opposites. Cupid and Anteros kept mortal love interesting, and Harmonia and the twins made sure neither peace nor panic stayed too long in the mortal mind.

He wondered if Aphrodite and Ares had abandoned their mission and had snuck away for a little "something-something."

Hold on, he thought, focusing in on Jen's prayers. Now she was asking if Therese was dead. Pete had seen her ghost in the woods. If Hip could help Than reunite Therese's soul with her body, he'd have less work and make his brother grateful all in one fell swoop. He god traveled back to the Underworld, deposited the souls he'd accumulated so far with Charon, and, without telling anyone, decided to take a brief reprieve from soul sucking to call on his mortal girl and her brother.

Twenty minutes later, he sat behind the wheel of a red Ford Mustang convertible speeding down the country road toward Lemon Reservoir. He couldn't very well arrive without any sign of transportation. There'd be explanations to make and excuses to give, and Hip didn't want any part of that. He couldn't help it if he had to take measures to blend in with the other occupants of the Upperworld. Might as well do it in style.

Chapter Four: Reunions

Therese and her parents sat on Therese's old bed in her childhood room, now oddly vacant compared to the days before she left to live in the Underworld over a year ago. The bed and dresser remained, but she had taken her desk, Jewels's tank, her flute and stand, some of the clothes from her closet, and two of the posters from her wall, along with the framed photo collage of her and Jen. She'd also taken most of her photo albums, but this earliest one, which her mom had made, Therese kept beneath her bed so she could look at it when she visited.

She and her parents flipped through the pages of the photo album. The family photos sparked happy memories and made them less aware of the other ghosts occupying the room. Their happiness was briefly sobered by Therese's explanation of her parents' murder by McAdams and his men, but they were pleased to learn the details of Therese's immortality.

"Clifford's immortal now, too," Therese added.

"Really?" her father laughed.

Her mother smiled. "Where is Clifford now?"

Therese bit her bottom lip. "I'm not sure. Hopefully, he's with Than."

She told them about how she met Hypnos and Thanatos while she was in a coma, and how Than had come to the Upperworld to get to know her. She told them how they fell in love and what a

40

kind and caring god Than was. She told them about the deal he had made with his father, and how, in the end, she couldn't kill another human being, especially a defenseless one.

"That's how we raised you," her father said with admiration, and then leaned his ethereal lips to her transparent forehead.

She thought she felt the ghost of his kiss, and though she longed for more, was grateful. If she'd been capable of crying tears, they would have been falling down her cheeks by now.

She told them about Vicki's mom and what had happened when she and Vicki took the ketamine. Therese felt ashamed to admit her role in Vicki's death, but also somewhat liberated by the confession. She also told them all about carrying the black box of beauty from Aphrodite to Persephone, stealing the apple from Hera's garden, which was guarded by the one-hundred-headed serpent, and navigating through the labyrinth where the Minotaur dwelled. Here she explained that the Minotaur, Asterion, and his sister, Ariadne, were actually good friends of hers.

"I visit them every chance I get," she added. "As the goddess of animal companions, I help Asterion by driving my arrows into the hearts of the visitors who plan to do him harm. Some people think it somehow proves their manliness if they can kill poor Asterion. And since he's part animal, my arrows make the intruders really fond of him. They even pet him like I do Clifford." She giggled, recalling one man who had wanted to stay and play fetch in the palace ruins of Knossos on the island of Crete for as long as he could. Therese had been left with no choice but to ask Phobos and

41

Deimos to get the man to leave. The twins had been happy to oblige.

"So you're the Minotaur's protector?" her mother asked.

"I suppose I am," Therese replied.

Therese then went on to tell about her adventure with the Hydra.

"You actually baked it a cake?" her father asked.

"The Hydra's a *she*, Dad. Not an *it*." Therese insisted. "And yes. And she loved it. But things didn't go as planned."

She went on to tell them about riding on the Hydra's back and plunging into the sinkhole.

"We're friends now, but back then, we terrified one another," Therese added.

She then told about the final challenge in the Underworld and how stupidly she had failed. "In the end, I couldn't stop myself from looking back."

"So how did you become a god?" her mother asked.

Therese told them about Demeter's method, and her parents gaped.

"You're not serious," her father said.

"And Than poured kerosene all over himself, and then held me until it was over."

"How horribly morbid!" her mother cried.

"He suffered because he loves me," Therese insisted.

"But burning alive? Was that really necessary?" her father asked.

42

"Unfortunately, yes," Therese said. "But it was totally worth it."

"Wasn't it painful?" her mother asked.

"Excruciatingly," Therese said. "The worst I've ever experienced."

"You must really love this boy," her father said.

This comment should have made Therese smile, but instead she frowned, and although she had no body, she felt her phantom heart tighten in her phantom chest. Before she could share with her parents the awful doubts about Than that had taken root and festered within her psyche, an earth-shattering shriek filled the room and caused every spirit present to howl in agony, including Therese and her parents.

***

Than flew above Canada with the siphon fashioned by his father and Hephaestus, gathering the souls into the device and wondering if they could feel anything, especially since there were so many of them compressed together in one small space. Unlike the souls who were presently dying, which he could sense and with whom he could communicate, these lost souls were disconnected to him in every way. If he could sense them, his quest to find Therese would be a cinch.

As it was, another of his disintegrated selves combed the woods near Therese's house, wondering if her attachment to her childhood home might have called her spirit back, as he'd seen happen to other ghosts who, for some reason or other, could not or would not enter the gates of the Underworld. Sometimes spirits were unleashed by powerful malevolent forces who managed to deceive Hades and his family. Invariably, those loosed spirits found their way back to their mortal dwellings.

Than wandered along the path through the woods to the house now belonging to Therese's aunt and uncle. He could hear Lynn's cries before he saw her, wrapped in a blanket in her mother's arms. The house was haunted by at least fifty ghosts, but so far, none was Therese.

He started up the stairs toward Therese's old bedroom. He wondered now whether her reluctance to marry him had more to do with missing her mortal family than with not loving him enough. Maybe it was a combination.

Whatever the cause, he hadn't seen it coming.

He tried not to think about it because it hurt too much.

When he reached the top step, he entered Therese's bedroom to find her seated on the edge of her bed between the souls of her parents. Although he could not hear what they were saying to one another, he could see them deeply engaged with one another and recognized that Therese's parents must have recovered at least some of their memory. This made him frown, because he was sure a second separation from them would be less bearable than the first. And there would have to be a second separation. Therese must know that if there were a way for her to be with her parents, he would have helped her to make it happen by now. Bonding with them again in this ghostly state was going to do none of them any good.

Before he could think much more about the second round of grieving Therese would have to endure, a familiar shriek resounded off the walls and caused the souls to howl.

***

Dusk was settling across the valley when Jen noticed a set of headlights turn up the gravel drive toward the Melner Cabin. Pete jumped up from his rocking chair.

"That him?" he asked.

"I guess." She got up, too.

It wasn't too dark to see it was Hip. He parked, grabbed the keys, and hopped from the car with the grace of a jackrabbit. Then he sauntered up the deck stairs as though he were aware of his audience. Whatever had made him leave in such a hurry must be behind him now.

"Hello," he said as he topped the steps.

"Everything alright?" Pete asked. "You left pretty quick."

"Family emergency," Hip said, crossing the wooden deck to lean on one of the rails overlooking the valley. "My dad was out of town, but now he's got everything under control."

"What happened?" Jen asked.

Hip continued to gaze out at the reservoir and the mountains on the other side. "I won't bore you with the gory details."

"We're worried about Therese," Pete said. "Can you get us in touch with your brother?"

Hip spun around to look at Pete. "Worried? Why?"

Pete pulled off his cowboy hat and played with it, like he often did when he was nervous. He averted his eyes. Jen wondered if he'd tell Hip the truth. "I got a bad feeling."

Hip took a few steps closer to Jen and her brother and studied Pete with narrowed eyes. Although her brother was tall and well-built, the new handler was at least an inch taller and thicker all around. "What kind of bad feeling?"

"A really bad feeling," Pete said. "Like something's happened to her. Like she could be…dead."

"We want you to call your brother," Jen said. "We aren't leaving here until you do." She held up her chin to let him know she wasn't backing down.

The new handler had the gall to smirk. Jen wanted to slap the expression right off his face.

"Is that a threat or a promise?" he said with a wink.

She felt the blood rush to her cheeks, but she refused to look away. "You can take it however you want."

To her relief, he slipped a cell phone from his back pocket. "Before I call my brother, I have a question for Pete."

Pete looked up at him. "Shoot."

"Are you a seer?"

"A what?" Pete asked.

"A seer."

"What's a seer?" Jen asked.

"A person who can see ghosts," Hip replied. "A seer can use ghosts to find out about the future."

Pete looked at Jen, but Jen didn't know what to tell her brother. She sure as heck wasn't going to say anything. If Pete saw ghosts, he was the one who'd have to decide if he was going to share it with others.

"Are *you*?" Pete asked Hip.

Hip chuckled. "I'm not exactly a seer, but I do see them."

Jen's mouth dropped open and Pete started talking a mile a minute.

"They're everywhere. Mostly Indians. But I saw Therese," Pete said. "Does that mean she's…"

"No," Hip said. "No, Therese is fine."

Jen was surprised by Hip's change in demeanor from arrogant jerk to someone kind and…comforting. "Are you sure? How do you know?" she asked.

"I just spoke with Than, when I was checking on my family emergency. Therese is fine. I'll tell her to call you. I think she and Than are tied up this evening."

Jen put her hands on her hips and squared herself to the new handler. "I thought you said the wedding was off. Why doesn't she come back home?"

"I'll let her explain that to you," Hip replied. Then he turned to Pete. "You okay, man?"

Pete nodded. "Just glad Therese is okay."

Hip slapped Pete on the shoulder in a friendly gesture, saying, "Good," and Jen felt a ripple of jealousy crawl down her back. She wanted Hip to pat her on the shoulder, too.

"See you in the morning?" Pete asked.

"I'll be there," Hip said, and gave Jen another wink.

She rolled her eyes as she made her way down the steps, but secretly felt elated. *You can wink at me all you like, mister,* she thought.

***

As Hip watched the girl walking away from him, admiring her curves and chuckling over the prayer she'd unwittingly sent to him—*You can wink at me all you like, mister*—he was distracted by a sound he at first mistook for the howling of wolves. But soon the ghosts wandering around the Melner cabin took up the same terrifying call, and a light went off inside his brain.

Melinoe.

Melinoe the Malevolent, she'd come to be called by Hip and his family. Even Persephone, the last one to hold out on believing in the existence of a redemptive quality in her daughter, had finally found Melinoe repugnant. It was impossible to love something so vile and cruel.

Some*thing,* not some*one.* Hip hardly considered her a person anymore. She was a wicked, evil thing who wreaked havoc on earth by tormenting lost souls and driving mortals insane.

Had she been behind the attack on the Underworld? It certainly provided her with an opportunity to harness more ghosts for her nightmarish antics, but Hip doubted she could pull off such a formidable attack on her own. If she were involved and not merely benefiting from it, she must have combined forces with another.

48

As Hip watched Pete and Jen pull away in Pete's pick up, he heard Jen's prayers to him change from flirtatious to frightened.

What is that howling, Hip? I have a feeling you know more than you're letting on.

He hoped he'd have a chance to visit her again tonight in her dreams, as he had nearly every night in the course of a year, but Melinoe's command of the ghosts in this area had him worried. He sent a prayer out to Than.

Do you hear that, bro? Hip prayed.

Melinoe is near, Than replied. *I need your help before I lose Therese forever.*

Chapter Five: Melinoe the Malevolent

As soon as Than heard the howling of the lost souls, he knew his estranged sister was near, working her evil. He'd abandoned Canada and brought the siphon to Therese's old room, and though he could not multiply the device, he disintegrated into twenty so that he might herd the spirits toward it. He hoped to save as many souls in the area as possible from the clutches of Melinoe the Malevolent.

Therese and her parents were among them, but Therese was resisting his attempt to rescue her. Unable to break free from Melinoe's call, she continued to howl along with the other ghosts, but unlike them, she recognized him and saw what he was doing.

"Don't run from me," he cried as he followed her and her parents from her room into the woods, which were dark with nightfall. "Come with me before it's too late!"

"Noooo!" she howled. "I don't want tooooooo! They know-ow-ow-ow meeeee!"

"You don't understand," he said, pointing his siphon toward them only to be evaded again. "They're in danger. So are you!"

He took as many souls as he was able while trying to persuade Therese to cooperate, but she and her parents continued to flee up the mountain as they howled. Than followed a few more feet and then stopped in his tracks. Several yards away, past the evergreens and Cypresses, in a clearing directly above him, stood Melinoe with her asymmetrical eyes, one white and the other black, fixed on his.

In each hand, one white and the other black, she held multiple whips, and on the ends of each whip were five to ten souls trapped in the leather straps like the victims of a group of octopi. Altogether, she had acquired at least fifty new ghosts to add to her menagerie.

And Therese and her parents were running straight for her.

With a roar louder than the howls of all the souls combined, Than disintegrated into a massive army and attacked his monstrous sister, unfurling her fists until the whips were dropped. Hip arrived in time to see Than whisk the Malevolent away from the woods and across the evening sky—all the way across the earth into the darkness of Greece. On the southernmost tip of Greece at Cape Matapan were the ruins of Poseidon's old temple beside an abandoned lighthouse. Beneath the lighthouse was a cave that once served as an entrance into the Underworld. When Hades banished Melinoe to the cave, he had sealed off the gates. The army of Thans now returned Melinoe to her cave where Hades awaited them.

"Hello, *Father*," she hissed with an ironic emphasis on "Father."

Half of her face was smooth and black, and the other was white and misshapen. On the white side of her face was the black eye, and on the black side, the white. Her black arm was also smooth, like a slender eel, but the skin of the white arm hung loose in places and was spotted with hairy moles. The hair on her head was parted down the middle and each side of the part matched the side of the

51

face it framed, so that whenever you saw her profile, depending on which way she was turned, she looked either all black or all white. It wasn't until you faced her square on that you saw her duality.

"You stopped being my daughter long ago," Hades said.

"And even way before that!" she growled. "Back and back and back and back and back!"

"Silence!" Hades roared. "Tell me who was in league with you against my kingdom and why."

Melinoe laughed. Then, along with her laughter, she repeated her mantra of, "Back and back and back and back and back!"

***

The screeching in Therese's phantom ears, which had caused her to wail, finally stopped. She backed away from Than toward her parents' souls, assessing the situation. She wasn't sure what had just happened, but she was certain Than wanted to return her parents to the Underworld.

"They remember me!" she said to him in the woods outside her home. "If you take them back, they'll forget me all over again!"

Than lowered the strange gun in his hands and took a step back. Was he leaving her?

"Don't go," she said.

"I'm not going anywhere," he said.

She could tell he was still hurt from earlier that day, when she'd announced for the third time that she was moving in with Hecate. She hadn't meant to hurt him, and her phantom heart tightened in her chest.

"You don't understand," he said. He was kind but aloof. "Unbound souls are in danger of becoming enslaved. If we leave your parents to roam the earth, Melinoe will capture them and…"

"Why didn't you ever tell me you had another sister?" Therese demanded. She couldn't stop herself.

"Therese, what's going on?" her father asked.

"This is Thanatos," Therese explained. "He's the god of the dead."

The souls of her parents looked at one another, then at Than, and then back to Therese.

"I thought you were in love with him," her mother said.

If Therese would have had blood in her cheeks, she would have blushed. "Mom, the point is that he wants to return you to the Underworld, where you've been all this time."

Her father narrowed his transparent eyes and asked, "And that's bad because?"

"Because you'll forget everything about your mortal life," Therese huffed. "You'll forget me."

"But what was this business about becoming enslaved?" Therese's mother asked.

Than stepped forward. "It's not safe for souls to wander the Upperworld. They're unprotected. Melinoe is just one of many deities who've been known to enslave mortal souls and use them to drive humans insane."

"Why would she do such a thing?" Therese asked.

Than shrugged. "No one understands her. Something happened to her while my mother was pregnant with her. My mother never speaks of it."

"But that's not Melinoe's fault," Therese objected.

Than shook his head. "Look, don't you think we tried for centuries to help her? Don't you think we tried everything possible?"

Therese opened her mouth to say something, but instead, it hung open. Finally she said, "I'm sorry. I didn't mean to suggest…"

"What's important right now is that I get all of you back to safety," Than said.

Therese felt a panic welling inside of her. "Wait! Just hold on!" She looked at her parents on either side of her and then pleaded with Than. "Let me have a few days more with them. I beg of you!"

Hip appeared beside Than. "It's not safe. You just don't' get it."

"No." She narrowed her eyes at the god of sleep. "I guess I don't."

"Then let me explain it to you in ways that are too unkind for my brother," Hip said, moving closer. "Melinoe will get inside your head and cause you to howl uncontrollably. While you are distracted, she will take you with her whip. Then she will drain you of any residual free will you once possessed and turn you into a vicious ghoul. You may retain your mortal memories," he continued, moving closer, his face inches from hers and possessing a cruel and frightening expression that made Therese take a step back, "but those memories will only make you more miserable as you helplessly victimize everyone you love who still lives on this earth. Do you want to see your aunt and uncle, or worse, your baby sister, tormented by you and your parents until they grow so mad they're locked up in an institution for the insane? And what about Pete and Jen and the other members of the Holt family? Well, that's what would happen, Therese. Every minute you stand here and wait, you make yourself and your parents susceptible to that evil thing we can hardly stand to call our sister. So forgive us for never mentioning her before. You see, each time we say or hear her name, it makes us want to puke."

Therese hardly knew what to say as she looked back at Hip with wide eyes.

"I've got Melinoe in my custody right now," Than said gently as he moved beside his brother. "Go ahead and spend a few more hours with your parents. I'll come back for you when it's time to return."

Hip shook his head. "Sounds risky, bro, but this is your call."

"Thank you," Therese said, wanting badly to throw her arms around Than, but not wanting to give him any false hopes. "Thank you so much."

***

Hip left the woods of Colorado sucking up more souls with the siphon along the way, wishing again he could find some lesser god or goddess to do this boring, mundane work. What about that wind bag, Aeolus? It shouldn't be too hard for him, being the god of the gales, to carry around the contraption as he blows. Hip laughed at his little joke. *Yep. Aeolus, that wind bag, sure does blow.*

And what about Eos, or maybe the Muses? He hadn't heard any songs to the gods lately, so he expected the muse Polyhymnia had some time on her hands. And at least one of the fifty Nereids could help.

As he entertained himself with his complaints, Hip made his way back to Greece, where he had started. Since he was there, he could not stop himself from listening in at the southernmost tip to his father's interrogation of the Malevolent.

He shivered at the scratchy sound of her voice, which had been affected by the malformation of her head in the womb.

"Do what you like, *Father*. I have nothing more to say," the goddess of ghosts hissed.

"I'll learn the truth eventually," Hades reasoned. "Why not cooperate with me now and avoid my wrath?"

"You know you cannot hold me," Melinoe challenged. "You've tried enough times to know I have my ways."

"Or allies," Hades said. "And believe me, you misguided creature, this investigation will expose all. Once I learn the identity of your allies, I'll be better equipped to imprison you long-term."

"Your investigation will come up short. I have nothing to fear."

"You underestimate the strength of your sisters. And the Furies have at their disposal the help of Artemis and Apollo." Hades added, "Ah, here they are now."

Hip sensed the arrival of the Furies and the twin Olympians, who must have been summoned by Hades. He flew down to the cave's entrance to get a look at what was happening.

"Hypnos," his father said. "Enter."

"Just thought I might help," Hip said without letting on his embarrassment at having been caught out.

Hades made no reply but turned to Tizzie, whose wolf sat at her feet and whose hands pinned back the arms of Cybele. Meg helped Tizzie by flanking the other side of their prisoner, and her falcon, it seemed to Hip, looked ready to strike. Tizzie's serpentine hair came to life, and the animated snakes, like those of Medusa, hissed threateningly at Cybele.

The next words Hades spoke were tinged with disgust. "Why have you brought this detestable creature to me? Is she a suspect, then?"

Cybele replied in her manly voice, "Why are you Olympians so fearful of that which you do not understand?"

Hip supposed she was once again referring to the fact that she'd been born with both male and female parts, and was called Adgistis until someone tricked her into castrating herself. As Cybele, she'd gone wild and had no more dealings with the gods. Rumor had it that she drove humans insane in the same way the wine of Dionysus did the Maenads, but Hip had also heard that some believed she was the mother of all gods, the earth goddess Rhea, who'd been scorned and dethroned by Zeus, and was powerless to defend herself.

"She has information," Apollo declared.

57

"Which I'm not at liberty to share unless you grant me asylum," Cybele said.

Hip's mouth fell open. Why would Cybele need asylum?

As if Hades had read Hip's mind, he asked, "From whom?"

"First you must agree to provide it, and then I'll tell you from whom, but not before all of these others."

"Stop this!" Melinoe screeched. "You're making a terrible mistake!"

"Join with me, Melinoe," Cybele offered. "Together we can stand against him."

"Against whom?" Hades demanded.

Cybele looked to the Furies on either side of her. "I need a private audience with you, Lord Hades."

Hades cleared his throat. "Thanatos, deliver Melinoe to Mount Olympus where she will remain a prisoner until a hearing can be arranged. Artemis and Apollo, you may return with them."

The army of Thans dispatched with its prisoner in tow, followed by the Olympian twins.

"Alecto, make certain the gates to the Underworld from this location have not been breached."

Alecto vanished.

"Tizzie and Meg, help me transport Cybele to my private chambers for further questioning." Then he turned to Hip. "Back to your duties, Hypnos."

Hip soared away from the cave, sucking up ghosts along the way, and then he delivered his souls to Charon once more before returning to his duties as god of sleep. The instructions from his father had been clear: every twelve hours he must return to his duties so that the mortal population would not suffer too long from poor sleep.

He made his usual rounds, checking on any whose dreams needed mitigating, and then he sought the one he most longed to see, as he did every chance he could get.

People slept at different times all over the world. At any given minute during a twenty-four-hour period, some population of people slept. Hip's job might not be as time-consuming and odious as his brother's, but it did keep him busy, even if it amused him most of the time. So his father had made a deal with him. Hip could alternate twelve hours on duty and twelve hours off for two weeks while he got to know the mortal girl.

Of course, there was something Hades wanted in return.

***

Jen followed Pete and Bobby all around the outside of their house looking for coyotes or wolves or something to explain the loud howling that resonated throughout Lemon Reservoir and the San Juan Mountains around their home. Pete carried his shotgun and Bobby his BB gun and Jen a baseball bat. Their mother had been convinced it was the wind until she stepped outside and found the trees barely moving in the light breeze. Then she feared a tornado was coming and had opened every window in the house and had pulled her mattress from her downstairs master bedroom, instructing the kids to be ready to shield themselves with it in her bathroom. But when she'd turned on the Weather Channel, she could find nothing about a tornado warning.

Then, as suddenly as it had started, the howling stopped.

After all that howling and the talk about ghosts, it was hard for Jen to fall asleep. Therese's crown sat near her on the bedside table, reminding her of her best friend and what a drag it was not to be able to talk to her on a regular basis anymore. Although she was glad to hear the wedding was off, she hoped Therese wasn't depressed and would consider coming back home. Jen didn't have anything against Than; she just couldn't see how Therese could be ready for marriage when she was only eighteen years old.

Plus, she missed her friend.

Soon her thoughts drifted from Therese to the new horse handler. Hip was every bit as good looking as his brother, and in some ways—maybe it was his cocky attitude—he was more. Jen hoped Hip would be there to help with the horses in the morning, as he had said he would. She couldn't wait to see him again.

She closed her eyes and tripped on a root in the ground outside her house. When she regained her footing, she realized she was outside in nothing but her t-shirt and underwear. Although it was dark, the moon was full, and it shone through the canopy of trees directly on her like a spotlight.

So odd, she thought.

As she turned to make her way back toward the house, she found herself face to face with Hip. Heat rushed to her face, and she pulled her t-shirt down, mortified.

"Hello there," Hip said with an easy grin. "You're looking lovely this evening."

She looked down to see she'd stretched her shirt tightly over her breasts, so that she may as well have been nude. She let go of the hem and crossed her arms. "What are you doing here?"

"Looking for you," he said with a twinkle in his eye.

She swallowed hard as he cupped her face in his hands. Then she stopped breathing altogether as he pressed his lips against hers.

His mouth swept across her jaw and then softly sucked on her bottom lip. She had never been kissed this way except in her dreams.

When he lifted his head to look at her, all she could say, in a breathless whisper, was, "Wowza."

He gave her a delighted smile and kissed her again.

Chapter Six: Questions

Than took his prisoner to Mount Olympus and presented her to Zeus and the other gods at court. All were present save Hermes, who continued to serve Than's father in the Underworld. Even the statues of Athena, Hestia, and his mother had been brought to the hall and placed near their respective thrones. Than thought this was probably for the best, for Mount Olympus was the safest fortress in the world.

He wanted to remain to learn more about the investigation. He also had questions, especially about the goddesses who'd been turned to stone. How long before they would be returned to normal?

61

But as soon as he handed his prisoner over, Zeus dismissed Than, and so he left.

Meanwhile, one of him had remained in the woods outside of Therese's house to watch over the souls of Therese and her parents, who now sat on the wooden deck like they once did when alive. The Malevolent may be in custody, but there were other, lesser, deities who enslaved lost souls. Melinoe was the worst and most prolific of them, but Than didn't want to take any chances.

All of the other souls in the area had been safely returned to the Underworld. Than worked busily across the earth recovering the remaining spirits and delivering them, safe and sound, to Charon.

As the sun began to rise and night turned into day, Than reluctantly told Therese it was time to go. He could sense her body calling back its soul.

She left the wooden deck and stood before him with the saddest eyes he'd ever seen. "Is there nothing we can do to save them?"

He wished he could tell her anything but the truth. "Their bodies are long gone, Therese. There's nothing I can do. Unless…" An idea popped into his head, but it was outrageous.

"Unless what?" she asked, the excitement unmistakable on her face.

"Well, I could put their souls into something living, like a tree or a chipmunk. Do you think they'd want to live for all eternity in the body of something else?"

Therese's mouth stretched into a wide smile, and she circled her arms around Than. Although he couldn't feel them, he had to admit it felt good to be in her arms, even if they were translucent. On the other hand, he wanted so much more than gratitude from her. He wanted to know she still loved him, and that she had always loved him, and that she hadn't simply used him to get this very thing—her parents back.

"What about the souls belonging to whatever we put them into?" she asked, pulling away with a frown. "What would happen to them? We wouldn't have to kill anything, would we?"

Than loved this about Therese. As badly as she wanted her parents to live, she didn't want it at the expense of others, even trees and chipmunks.

"Most trees haven't developed souls," Than said.

"I'd hate for my parents to be stuck inside something that can't move around." She looked up at the branches overhead.

He followed her eyes to the branches above them and was struck by another idea. "We could wait until something like a bird is about to die, and just as I'm taking the soul of the bird out, we could put the soul of one of your parents in. Then you could give immortality to the bird."

Therese jumped up and down like a kangaroo. "Let me run it by my parents!"

***

When Therese saw Stormy standing in his stall chomping on a bit of hay, she rushed over to him and threw her arms around his neck. Clifford nudged her leg, feeling a little jealous, so she scooped him up in her arms.

"Are you two ready to go on some more missions with me?"

"Can we start yesterday?" Clifford barked, forever anxious for adventure.

"Let's go," Stormy brayed.

"Not yet," Therese said. "But soon."

From the stables, she went to Than's rooms to find Jewels and was relieved to find her tortoise safe in her tank. Therese moved the tank, along with Clifford's bed, to Hecate's chambers, not wishing to be separated from her pets again.

But even more wonderful was the feeling of having her parents perched in the bodies of two lovely cardinals on each of her shoulders. She gave her parents a tour of the Underworld and introduced them to everyone she knew. She told them all about her life as the goddess of animal companions and even took them on a couple of trips to save lost animals and bring humans and animals closer together. Therese rode on Stormy's back, with Clifford in the saddle in front of her and her parents perched on each of her shoulders. She didn't stay out long, still somewhat tired because of all that had transpired in the previous days, and she wanted to make sure Stormy was fully recovered.

After spending a few more days together in Hecate's rooms, she and her parents agreed it would be best if they returned to their home in Colorado to watch over Carol, Richard, and Lynn. It had been feeling crowded in Hecate's room with Galin and Cubie, to boot. Plus, the Underworld wasn't the most ideal place for birds. Therese would visit every chance she could get, and now that her parents were immortal, they could all three communicate with one another through prayer.

Therese had never been happier...sort of. No, she admitted. She *had* been happier. Just last year when she was planning to marry Than, she'd been the happiest she'd ever been. Even having her parents back couldn't top that feeling of euphoria. But once she'd come to actually live full time in the Underworld and had begun to learn more about the ways of the gods and goddesses, the feeling of euphoria had left her body like the air of a deflating balloon.

She returned to her duties as goddess of animal companions full time, having had neglected them for too long, and poured herself into her work, saving lost pets and bringing animals and humans together. As she speared the heart of a little girl passing through an animal shelter and saw her take the neglected puppy into her arms with profound love, Therese's mind wandered back to Than and how much she wished she could be with him forever.

After one week of straight work, Therese decided to take a break at Café Moulan in Paris, sure that a coffee and Danish were just what she needed to lift up her spirits. She presented herself in mortal form with her quiver and bow invisible, so as not to disturb the patrons out on the sunlit patio. As she passed one of the umbrellas at a corner table, she recognized Aphrodite sitting alone with a glass of juice.

Therese said hello silently, through prayer, and Aphrodite beckoned her over.

"I don't want to disturb you," Therese said. "I can eat over there if you'd like to be alone." Therese gestured at an empty table across the patio.

"I never like to be alone," Aphrodite said, which was hard for Therese to understand, because Therese often craved alone time, and it was becoming less and less possible to have now that she was a god. "Please, sit down. I've wanted to talk with you for some time, and this will give me that chance."

Therese took the chair across from Aphrodite. The waiter immediately came up beside them to take down Therese's order, and once he left, Aphrodite leaned across the table.

"Tell me the truth. Why have you postponed your wedding?"

Therese felt the blood rush to her face. Except for Than, the goddess of love was the first to demand an explanation.

As Therese struggled to come up with an answer, Aphrodite asked, "You still love him. I can feel it. In fact, your love for one another is as strong as any I've ever known."

Tears welled up in Therese's eyes. "Does he still love me, then?" she asked, as a desperate mortal might a fortune teller.

"Why would you doubt it?"

"Because I've hurt him." Therese leaned in closer and said. "I've told him I don't want to marry him. Ever."

   ***

Hip had been working for the Holts for nearly a week, and he still hadn't found a way to maneuver the mortal girl into his bed. He'd had plenty of fun with her in the Dreamworld, but in the

Upperworld, as they brushed and rode horses, shoveled hay, and removed tack, Jen kept her distance. One afternoon, after Pete and Bobby had gone to ride in the mountains and Mrs. Holt had gone into the house to cook lunch, Hip had a rare moment alone with Jen in the barn. She was putting the brushes away when he came in from turning out the last of the horses. Her arms stretched up to set the brushes up on a high shelf, and he stood there, enjoying the curves of her profile. It was now or never, he thought to himself as he crossed the barn and lifted her face to his.

Just as he had done every night in her dreams, he cupped her face in his hands and pressed his lips to hers. The taste of her lips was exquisite—even better than he had imagined. The feel of her warm breath against his made the hair on the back of his neck tingle with pleasure. He expected her to close her eyes and melt against him as she always did, but instead, she bit his lip, stomped on his foot with her boot, and shoved him back with both hands.

"What do you think you're doing?" she asked.

He hardly knew what to say. "I, I…"

"Maybe other girls let you get away with treating them like that, but I'm not like other girls." She made to leave the barn, but he grabbed her arm when she passed him.

"What did I do wrong?" he asked, fighting the blush of humiliation that threatened to spread into his cheeks. He'd been pushed away plenty of times by girls, but this time, it actually hurt, and not just physically.

"Not one text or phone call for a year, and then you expect you can just waltz up to me and…"

"But…"

She must have read the confusion and disappointment on his face, because she seemed to soften as she looked up at him and said, "You can't expect to kiss a girl like that before you've even taken her out to dinner."

He let go of her arm, as both the blush and relief swept over him. "So that's how it works, hmm? I feed you, and then I get to kiss you?"

To his profound relief, she smiled back. "Something like that."

"What time should I pick you up?"

"I'm busy tonight," she said as the corners of his mouth drooped. "But I'm free tomorrow. I suppose I can eat with you then."

Before he could say another word, she turned on her heels and left the barn.

All he could think to say as he spoke beneath his breath was, "Wowza."

***

Jen smiled as she left the barn, quite pleased with herself. Let him suffer one night, she thought as she entered the house. She didn't have any plans, of course, but she didn't want to come across as easy. If he wanted to kiss her again, she'd make him work for it.

She washed her hands at the kitchen sink and helped her mom with the lunch preparations, all the while unable to keep the smile from her face.

"What are you so happy about?" her mother asked.

"Nothing."

She'd been dreaming about him since he took her to the movies a year ago. They'd had a nice time together—at least she had thought so—and she'd even let him give her a little kiss on the lips. He had wanted more, but she wasn't that kind of girl. When he never called her again, she thought he didn't like her.

But he came back, and now it seemed his main reason for coming back was to see her.

"Watch what you're doing," her mother scolded when Jen dropped the spoon all the way down into the gravy. "Now you'll have to fish it out with another."

That night, Jen looked forward to dreaming again of Hip. The dreams were always so real. In fact, today, in the barn, she got the strange feeling that he'd been dreaming of her, too, and that, somehow, he knew she'd been dreaming of him.

She tripped on a stair in her high school. Hip reached out his strong arms and caught her and kept her from falling.

"Hello, there," he said with a grin that wasn't as easy as usual. "Watch your step."

"There was something I was going to ask you," she said. "But I can't remember what it was."

"Maybe you were going to ask me to kiss you again, like I did today in the barn."

Jen pinched her brows together. "Wait a minute."

"You've never stopped me before," he said, moving his mouth closer to hers.

"But I did stop you. I stopped you today. But, wait a minute." She fought to bring up the memory. "I wasn't dreaming then! So that means…"

"It's about time." He smirked.

Other students walked up and down the stairs, distracting Jen and making it difficult for her to keep track of what it was she was figuring out. "Can we go someplace more private?"

Instantly, she found herself with him in the barn.

"I'm not just a figment," he said, taking her hand. "It's really me. Try to remember this tomorrow. Try to remember all the times we've already kissed, all the nights we've spent together."

"Only dreams," she said.

"Why are dreams any less real?"

"Are you saying you are dreaming of me, too? Are we sharing this dream?"

"Indeed we are. Ask me about it tomorrow."

"How can I remember? What if I don't?"

He took the pink scarf she was wearing around her neck. "I'll bring this to you tomorrow. Maybe it will help you to recall."

Then, without further ado, he leaned in and gave her the kiss he'd wanted to give her earlier that day, and this time, since it was only a dream, she let him.

Chapter Seven: Revelations

Aphrodite raised her eyebrows in surprise. "Why ever not, Therese? After all you've been through together? He's going to suffer at the hands of the Maenads once a year forever, and now you won't marry him?"

Therese was silent as the waiter served her coffee and a Danish. Then, when they were alone again, Therese took a sip of the hot liquid and licked her lips as she tried to think of the right words to explain her feelings. The early morning sun offered her no suggestions.

Therese asked, "Are you happy, Aphrodite?"

"Me? Of course I'm happy. Why would you ask me that?"

"Because you're married to Hephaestus when you obviously have a thing for Ares," Therese said bluntly, feeling the blood rush to her cheeks. "I'm sorry. I shouldn't..."

"No, don't apologize," Aphrodite said, averting her eyes. "It's true."

"So I've decided to be like Athena and Hestia."

"Frigid?"

"Well, not literally," Therese said. "I'm sorry, that wasn't funny. What's the progress there, anyway? Are we any closer to freeing them and Persephone?"

"Last I heard, Zeus managed to transform Hestia back to normal, but there was a powerful ward around Athena and

Persephone that no one, not even Zeus, can touch. Even Ares is baffled by it."

Therese took a bite of her Danish.

"Listen, to me, Therese," Aphrodite said gently. "Not everyone is called to love romantically, and Athena and Hestia are two examples of persons who are happiest without passionate entanglements. But you aren't like them. You are more like me. I can feel your passion emanating from you. You can't deny it."

Therese didn't know what to say.

"Do you deny it?" Aphrodite asked.

Therese shook her head. "But I don't want Than to marry me and then, centuries later, fall in love with another, like what's happened with you and Ares. Eternity is too long for romantic love, I guess."

"But, Therese…"

"No, listen, I've asked around. I've done research. Every single god who has married has at one time or another cheated on his wife. Even *your* husband, who seems the most loving and faithful of all, has had children with another woman."

Aphrodite glanced around and then said, "Lower your voice."

Therese took a deep breath. "I'm so sorry."

"You've got it all wrong about Hephaestus and me," Aphrodite said.

"What do you mean?"

"I never loved him. It was always Ares. See, when Hephaestus was born, Hera thought she'd been tricked and that a monster had been switched with her child, because she'd never before seen a malformed god. She threw her baby from Mount Olympus. Hephaestus was rescued and raised by Thetis and Eurynome in a cave on a riverbank. When he grew older, he wanted to get back at his mother for never trying to find him once she learned the truth. He sent her a golden throne."

"I've heard this," Therese interrupted. "Hera was trapped on the throne, and Zeus offered you as the bride to whoever could free her."

"Exactly. We all expected it to be Ares. Even Zeus was certain his strong and brilliant son would be our savior, though I've had my doubts about Zeus's motives."

"You once told Than that Zeus married you off to Hephaestus to make you unhappy, so it would diminish your beauty."

"Yes. That's my theory," Aphrodite said. "But at the time, I was sure Ares would be the one to save Hera. He was the only one I thought would come forward. Everyone else was glad for Hera to be stuck on the throne."

Therese and Aphrodite shared a laugh at Hera's expense.

Aphrodite continued, "But Dionysus gave Hephaestus the idea to come himself, so Hephaestus could claim me, and because Zeus had sworn on the River Styx, I was stuck."

Therese's eyes widened at this revelation. "So you never loved Hephaestus?"

"No. And he never truly loved me. He didn't really know me," Aphrodite explained. "He's been kind to me all these years, and I have grown to care for him, but the passion you feel for Than is like that which I have always felt for Ares."

"But Zeus, Poseidon, and Hades—they've all cheated on their wives."

"They're the most powerful gods among us, and their temptations are also greater. I'm not excusing their behavior, mind you. But Than won't be subjected to the same level of temptation as the lords of the sky, sea, and earth."

"But…"

"I want to tell you one more thing, Therese," Aphrodite said, "and not many know this."

"I'm listening."

"You must swear on the River Styx to tell no one."

"I swear."

"Hephaestus and I were granted a secret divorce by Zeus years ago."

"What?" Could Aphrodite be telling the truth? Therese wondered how she had never heard of this.

"It was after our divorce that he had affairs with two nymphs and then eventually married Algaia, the oldest of my Graces and the mother of all his divine children—well, except for one, but that's a long story."

"I…"

"So you see, he never cheated on anyone. Hephaestus is one god who has always been faithful."

Therese looked up at Aphrodite with surprise. She'd been convinced fidelity was impossible among the immortals, but here was Aphrodite throwing her a bone. "Seriously?"

"Yes."

***

Than stood outside Hecate's rooms but could not feel Therese's presence on the other side of the wooden door. She was still out. By his calculations, she'd been gone from the Underworld for at least a week without a break. Before he could god travel back to his chambers, the wooden door opened, and Hecate greeted him on the other side of the threshold.

"Looking for Therese?" she asked.

He nodded.

"Haven't seen her in days, but she prayed to me this morning that she'd be coming home to rest this afternoon. I think she needs some sleep."

"Please don't mention I stopped by," Than said through his dry throat.

"Are you sure?"

He nodded, thanked her, and was about to move on when Therese appeared beside them.

"Than?"

"Oh, hello, Therese." He was suddenly not sure where to put his hands. He swallowed hard. "How are you?"

She glanced at Hecate and gave her a smile. "I'll come visit with you and the girls in a bit, okay? I'm going to go talk to Than right now."

Hecate disappeared behind the wooden door, leaving Than and Therese alone in the corridor.

"You are?" he asked.

"If that's okay." She smiled up at him.

They went to his rooms and stood before the blazing fire in the hearth.

"Listen," he said when she took a step toward him. "You don't' have to do this."

She gave him a look of confusion, but continued toward him until her arms were wrapped around his neck. "Do what?"

He felt every atom of his body awaken as his arms wrapped around her waist of their own accord. He'd longed for this for months. But he didn't want payback. He wanted her to love him. "You don't have to…show your gratitude."

He felt her stiffen as she dropped her arms and searched his face. "Gratitude?"

His throat tightened. Her lips were so close to his. He wanted to shut up and kiss her. "For finding a way to save your parents. Isn't that what this is about?"

She backed away, and something inside him died.

"I thought you knew me better than that."

"Therese," he held out his hand. "I'm sorry. I don't understand."

She vanished.

Before he could follow her, a knock came at his door. He sensed Meg on the other side.

"Enter."

Meg's face looked paler than usual in stark contrast to the black falcon perched on her shoulder.

"Something's gone wrong on Mount Olympus," she said.

He waited for her to explain.

"Melinoe the Malevolent has escaped."

***

Hip appeared in Jen's bedroom as Jen slept in the early morning dawn. She looked lovely with her blonde hair fanned across her pillow and her long lashes resting on her soft white cheeks. Her lips were slightly open. He leaned close to her face and breathed in her earthly scent. He wished the senses in the Dreamworld were as potent as they were here. He brushed his lips gently on her forehead before plucking her pink scarf from the hook behind her door and vanishing from the room.

A few hours later, when he entered the barn, all but Pete were there brushing the horses.

"Nice scarf," Bobby teased.

"Thanks," Hip said with a wink.

Jen turned from her mare and gawked at him.

"Mornin', Hip," Mrs. Holt said from across the barn.

"Good morning, ma'am." He took a step toward Jen. "Good morning, Jen."

Jen backed up against her mare, still gawking. Then she clutched her head with both hands.

Hip frowned. Maybe she wasn't ready for this. "Are you okay?"

"I, I…"

"What's wrong, Jen? You seeing ghosts now, too?" Bobby teased.

Mrs. Holt came up alongside her daughter. "Jen? Are you having one of your attacks?"

"I can't breathe," Jen said. "I need air."

Jen stumbled from the barn, through the gate of the pen, and up the steps to the wooden deck of the house.

Hip and Mrs. Holt followed. Pete came out of the house and asked what was wrong.

"She's having one of her panic attacks." Mrs. Holt helped Jen onto a chair. "Go get me a wet rag."

Pete disappeared behind the front door and returned moments later with a wet towel, which Mrs. Holt pressed against her daughter's forehead.

"Take deep breaths, baby." Mrs. Holt crouched beside her daughter's chair. "Let them out slowly, like the doctor said."

Hip felt like dirt, and he prayed to his old girlfriend, Pasithea, for help. *I need you, Pasithea.*

The goddess of relaxation appeared beside him as a bright orb, which he hid from the eyes of the mortals with a blanket of invisibility.

The effect Pasithea had on the mortals was immediate. Jen's breaths slowed down, her hands stopped trembling, and she looked up at him with sleepy eyes. Mrs. Holt dropped into the chair beside Jen with a heavy sigh.

"Thanks, Mom," Jen said. "That cold rag helped."

"Why don't we take the day off today?" Mrs. Holt said lazily. "I expect one day won't hurt none. If you're okay, Jen, I think I'll go lie down."

"I'm okay now," Jen murmured.

"I'll go tell Bobby," Pete said. "We'll feed them and then turn them out." Pete climbed down the wooden steps and went inside the barn.

Pasithea narrowed her eyes at Hip. He silently thanked her and promised he owed her one. As awkward as it felt asking for her help, he was relieved to see Jen calm. Pasithea cast jealous eyes on Jen and disappeared in a dust devil. The mortals noticed, but did not react.

"You okay?" Hip asked Jen.

"Where did you get my scarf?" she asked, sitting up in her chair.

"I told you last night I'd wear it as a sign," he said, hoping she wouldn't panic again.

He took the scarf from around his neck, knelt on the deck beside her, and then wrapped the scarf around her. "It looks better on you."

"Who are you?" she asked, trembling again.

"The boy from your dreams," he whispered.

"Wait," she gasped. "Did you say the boy *of* my dreams?"

"The boy *from* your dreams," he said again. "But I'd like to be both."

"How is this possible?" she whispered. "Am I dreaming now?"

"Come on." He stood and held out his hand. "I want to show you something."

***

Jen's knees weakened beneath her as she took the steps down from the house and followed the boy across the gravel drive and into the road.

"Where are we going?" she asked, still not sure whether she was awake or asleep.

"Just walk with me awhile."

With her hand in his, he led her across the road and through the tall grass toward the lake. The sun climbed from behind her house toward the sky and shone brightly on their backs, but Jen was shivering, her teeth chattering, though she wasn't cold.

"You remember how I told Pete I could see ghosts, too?" he asked.

She tried to nod. She may or may not have succeeded.

"The reason I can see them is because I'm a god—the god of sleep, to be precise."

Jen stopped in her tracks, like a chipmunk in the road. "Don't joke with me. I don't feel well."

"I'm serious." He squared himself to her. The sun reflected in his bright blue eyes and dark blond hair. "Don't you remember me from your dreams?"

"So I've had a few dreams about you," she stammered. "That doesn't prove anything."

He lifted her chin and studied her face, sending shocks through her whole body. "I hate to say it, but maybe this was a mistake."

She arched a brow. "What?"

"You can't handle the truth." He dropped his hand and stepped away, gazing out at the lake.

Jen didn't like being told she couldn't handle something. She might have panic attacks now and then, and it was true that snakes and spiders gave her the willies, but she was a strong person and she could handle just about anything.

"Why should I believe you're a god?" she demanded.

"Because it's true. Humans, plants, and animals aren't the only living beings in existence. Why is that so hard for mortals to grasp?"

"If you told me you were an alien, like a Martian or something, it would be easier to believe," Jen snapped.

"Every aspect of the world or humanity is served by the gods. There's a god or goddess for love, peace, war, hate, wisdom, healing, the sea, the sky, the underground—you name it. I'm the god of sleep."

If Hip was a god, his brother was, too, and that explained a lot about what was happening with Therese. It also explained the crown. It was the crown that finally helped her to at least try to believe.

"Never mind," Hip said with a sigh. "You're one of those mortals who can't handle the truth."

"I can, too," she insisted, though her chattering teeth might have indicated otherwise.

He turned and sought her eyes. She was surprised by the smile that stretched across his face. He held out his hand, and she took it, though her own hand was trembling like a drug junkie in need of a fix.

"The god of sleep, huh?" she asked. "Then shouldn't I be falling asleep in front of you?"

"I'm not serving at this moment. I'm in mortal form. My godly form would be too much for your mortal eyes."

"Oooh. Too much for my eyes," she teased.

"It would kill you."

She looked him over from top to bottom. He sure was hot enough to be a god. "The god of sleep, huh?" she repeated. "So what does that make your brother?"

He gave her a wary glance. "The god of death."

She stopped again in her tracks as her mouth fell open. "But Therese…"

"Let me take you to her, okay?"

"To Therese?"

"If you can handle it, that is."

Jen sucked in her lips and squeezed his hand. She gave him a nod. "I can."

Chapter Eight: Mistakes

Tizzie appeared beside Meg in Than's chambers, her black serpentine hair hissing wildly. Blood mixed with tears and slid down her cheeks. Than rarely saw his sister looking so distraught.

"What is it?" Than asked.

"The Malevolent has breached the gates," Tizzie reported with a look of anguish on her face. "And she's just freed Medusa from my custody."

For a moment, Than thought he must be in the Dreamworld. This couldn't be possible otherwise.

"How could that happen?" Meg demanded.

"Her power overwhelmed me," Tizzie replied, unable to look her brother and sister in the eye. "She must have someone helping her."

Who would be working with the Malevolent?

Than squeezed Tizzie's shoulders. "Where's Father? He won't answer me."

"No one's supposed to know this," Tizzie started. "But he's gone to Mount Olympus to bring back Mother. Apparently Cybele said something during her interrogation that made retrieving Mother his first priority."

"Where's Cybele now?" Than asked.

"Alecto is with her in Father's sitting room," Tizzie replied.

Than disintegrated and dispatched to question Cybele. But to his sisters, he said, "*Our* priority is to recapture the Malevolent. Agreed?"

"Agreed," his sisters replied.

***

Therese fell on Hecate's bed, flat on her belly, and buried her face and cried.

Clifford jumped onto the bed and licked nervously at her ear. "What's happened?"

"Therese?" Hecate called from her comfy chair across the room. "Therese, honey, talk to us."

Therese rolled onto her side on the bed to see Hecate standing over her, Cubie's paws on the bedside, and Galin, who'd been napping near the bath, with her head stretched up in concern. Clifford nuzzled her hand with his head.

"I've ruined everything," Therese confessed. "Than doesn't think I love him." She covered her face and returned to her belly. She missed having her own room where she could have a good cry without an audience, without worrying about how she must look to others.

"Listen to me." Hecate sat on the edge of the bed. "You can't just lie here and cry about this. You can do something. Think about what company you're in."

Therese rolled over and sat up as Hecate continued, feeling even more pathetic.

"Look at my sweet polecat over there. All Galin wanted to do was help Alcmene deliver Hercules. Alcmene had been in labor for days. Hera had convinced the Fates to keep their arms crossed to prevent Hercules from being born, but poor Galin thought Alcmene would go mad with the labor pains. So Galin courageously deceived the Fates by announcing that a son had been born. The Fates held up their arms in surprise, and Hercules was born.

"The Fates were embarrassed when they learned of the deception, and they changed Galin into what she is today, but first they cut off her female parts and warned her that if she ever gave birth, it would be through her throat!" Hecate gritted her teeth. "To this day, I refuse to have anything to do with those three old gambling witches. But look at Galin. Even after all that, she's found a purpose here with me."

Therese shuddered, recalling her visit with the Fates last year. If she'd known what they were capable of, the cruelty...she shuddered again.

Galin jumped into her mistress's lap.

"We have a good life together, don't we, Galin?"

"Yes," the weasel said. "It made me sad to hear you retell my story, but if it hadn't happened, I wouldn't be with you. I'm happier than I've ever been."

Cubie moved closer to the pair and nudged Galin's paw. "The same goes for me."

"And you're next," Hecate said. "I hope that's alright with you, Cubie. You're story always brings you to tears."

"Go ahead and tell it," the Doberman said with a sigh.

Therese wiped her eyes, and Clifford climbed into her lap as they listened to Hecate.

"Cubie was once called Hecuba. And she was married to Priam, the King of Troy. They had—what was it, Cubie, nineteen children?"

"Yes. Nineteen."

"You've probably heard of them—Hector, Paris, Cassandra…"

"Oh, of the Trojan War?" Therese asked. "Like in *The Iliad* and *The Odyssey*?"

"That's right," Hecate said.

"I lost all of my children because of that war." Cubie's eyes flooded with tears.

Therese knew something about loss, but she couldn't imagine losing nineteen children. Plus, she'd read *The Iliad* and *The Odyssey* in her last year of high school, and she remembered how brutal the battle was and how valiantly Hector fought. She shuddered and wondered why people had to kill one another rather than negotiate a compromise.

"After the war, Odysseus took her as his slave," Hecate said. "And he was unkind to her."

Odysseus, unkind? Then again, back then, women were considered spoils of war. They were property that could be won and lost and bargained for.

"A god took pity on me and turned me into a dog, so I could fight back Odysseus and escape," Cubie said. "At first I was miserable and alone and afraid, but then Hecate took me in and showed me my daughter, Laodice, who'd been saved by Persephone. She lives down here with Lethe."

"The river goddess?" Therese asked.

"Yes," Cubie said. "Laodice was said to be my most beautiful daughter, and Lethe thinks so, too. They make each other happy. And I can visit them when we come to live here for the fall and winters."

"Therese, I'm telling you their stories so you can see how you can't let a little misunderstanding stop you from finding happiness. Galin and Cubie were able to make the most out of their hard times. You can, too."

Hecate was right: Therese was acting like a big baby. She needed to go back to Than and convince him that she really did love him, no matter what it took. As she was about to thank Hecate and leave, however, a knock came at the door, and Therese, sensing a mortal, dimmed her brightness, as all gods automatically did to protect mortal eyes. She and Hecate exchanged puzzled glances. Therese thought she sensed Jen, but she hoped she was wrong.

"What mortal would be at my door?" Hecate whispered.

"Dim yourselves," came Hip's voice from the corridor. "I have a mortal with me."

Therese wanted to say "Duh" to Hip for stating the obvious, but she held her tongue. Then in walked Hip and, as she had feared, Jen.

Therese jumped to her feet. Clifford went crazy with excitement, running up to meet Jen like he used to do.

Jen's mouth hung open and her eyes were wide with shock.

"Hip?" Therese said. "Are you kidding me? You brought Jen *here*?" Could Than's twin brother be any more foolish?

"T-T-Therese?" Jen asked with a terrified expression.

"Can you take her to the poppy fields and make her think this was all a dream?" Therese suggested. "What do you think this will accomplish?"

Jen's head jerked down to Clifford, whose paws were on her shins. "C-C-Clifford?"

"She wouldn't believe me when I told her I was a god," Hip explained.

"I can see why," Therese said, maybe a bit too harshly. "With the way you're acting, I can't believe it either!"

Hip narrowed his eyes into a look of anger he'd never shown Therese before. "Hold on right there."

Cubie walked over to Jen and said to Clifford, "Aren't you going to introduce us?"

At Cubie's gift of human language, Jen's eyes opened even wider. Therese worried they'd pop from their sockets. Jen looked from Cubie to Therese, and then fell forward in a faint.

***

Great, Hip thought. *Can this night get any worse?*

"What did you think would happen, Hip?" Therese asked. "That she'd say, 'Okay, I believe you now,' and throw her arms around you?"

"Something like that," he said. He sure didn't appreciate Therese's haughty attitude toward him. Who did she think she was? She was the new god on the totem pole, and she had better watch her step, as far as he was concerned. He lifted Jen up in his arms and laid her out on the bed. "What do you suggest I should have done?"

"Oh, I don't know. Anything but *this*!"

"Let's all calm down," Hecate said.

Hip's mind suddenly resounded with prayers from Meg and Tizzie, and a moment later the two Furies appeared in the room followed by Than.

"The Malevolent escaped Mount Olympus and has freed Medusa," Than announced. "Why are you dimmed?"

"Where are they?" Hip asked. So this night could get worse after all.

"We don't know," Meg said in a vicious voice. "Isn't that obvious?"

"Where's Hades?" Therese asked.

"Here," came Hades's voice as he appeared in the doorway with the statues of Persephone and Athena. "We have no time to lose. I need all of you to help me destroy the ancient ward surrounding my queen. And get that mortal out of here."

"How do we help?" Hip asked.

"Come with me to my sitting room where Cybele awaits us. She knows what to do."

Hades vanished with the statues in tow.

The Furies followed behind.

"What about Jen?" Therese asked. "Oh no! She's barely breathing. Than, get out of here!"

Thanatos vanished.

"We'll watch over her until you return," Cubie said, meaning her and the other animals.

"I'll be right back," Hecate reassured her dog.

Hip, Therese, and Hecate left Hecate's chambers and appeared on the scene with Cybele, who spoke in a manly voice, "This won't work without the eye of Polyphemus."

"You might have mentioned that before I assembled all the gods of the Underworld here," Hades reprimanded.

"You left in rather a hurry," Cybele stated. "You gave me no chance, Lord Hades."

"Father, can you explain what's going on?" Than asked.

"There's no time, son. Take Therese and your sisters to the Island of the Cyclopes and borrow Polyphemus's eye."

Hip and Hecate remained with Hades and the prisoner, Cybele. Hip noticed that he could no longer communicate with his mother and hadn't heard from her in some time.

"She continues to solidify," Hades explained. "We could soon lose her entirely."

"What would you have me do?" Hip asked.

"You and Hecate search for the Malevolent," Hades replied. "She can be anywhere."

***

Jen opened her eyes and saw she was in the middle of a big bed in a bright cave surrounded by two dogs and a weasel. She smiled when Clifford licked her arm, but as the memory of what had transpired moments before came flooding back, she frowned.

"Clifford, where am I?" Jen asked, not expecting an answer.

He barked—so far so good. But then the Doberman pinscher said, "You're in the Underworld."

Jen froze. She could not move, could not breathe, for several long seconds. The animals stared at her, and she stared at them. She didn't know what to think. She couldn't think. Her mind reeled.

Finally, she asked, "Am I dreaming?"

The animals looked at one another.

Then the weasel said, "Not at the moment."

Jen flinched and pushed her body further away from the animals. A talking Doberman was one thing, but the weasel talked, too?

"Don't be afraid," the Doberman said. "Hip and the others will come back for you soon."

"Therese?" she asked.

"Yes, Therese, too," the weasel said.

Jen looked at Clifford, and he barked.

"Are we, are we dead?" Jen asked. "Is this hell? Please don't tell me I've died and gone to hell." She glanced at the flames lighting up the room.

"You're not dead yet," said the weasel. "So relax. Your friends will be back soon."

Jen's eyes widened. Not dead yet? What was that supposed to mean? She bit down on her lip and clasped her hands together, trying to keep them still.

Suddenly the wooden door burst open and a strange looking woman who was half white and half black stormed into the room.

Chapter Nine: Cyclopes Island

As Therese flew across the predawn sky with Than and the Furies, she wondered how they were supposed to *borrow* the only eye of a Cyclops. Than had once told her the Cyclopes were cruel cannibals who'd been allowed to live because they forged Zeus's thunderbolts. She also knew that Odysseus and his men had once stabbed Polyphemus in the eye and blinded him, but of course, being immortal the eye of Polyphemus had regenerated. Why was *his* eye necessary to freeing the goddesses who'd been turned to stone by Medusa?

They flew west of Greece to a group of islands supposedly invisible to mortal eyes. Therese didn't know enough about world geography to know if she'd ever heard of the islands in her pre-god life. Who knew world geography would be one of her most important classes?

Her thoughts were interrupted by messages coming telepathically from Than and his sisters.

Polyphemus is dangerous, Than said.

Therese thought, "How stupid does he think I am?"

He lives in a cave with his flock of sheep, Than continued. *And every morning before he takes the sheep into the hills, he goes to the sea to wash his eye.*

He won't give us the eye willingly, Meg said. *We'll have to ambush him.*

We'll wait in the sea until he submerges the eye, Alecto offered.

Not the sea, Tizzie said. *Polyphemus is the son of Poseidon. Too risky.*

Well, we can't hide in the clouds, Than said. *The Cyclopes work for Zeus, and Zeus may sense us there.*

Wouldn't Zeus want to save the goddesses? Therese asked.

There's a reason my father brought them from Mount Olympus, Than replied. *I don't know what it is, but I don't think we can trust anyone right now. Not even Zeus.*

What a frightening existence being a god proved to be when you couldn't even trust your king.

A bolt of lightning shot through the sky and cut through a cloud in the center of the group. The gods scattered and plunged into the sea.

Therese held her breath, unused to underwater breathing. A school of fish darted away from her. She looked down and saw the ocean floor was hundreds of feet below her. *Talk about deep.*

Follow me, Thanatos said.

Even if Than hadn't been glowing like a beacon—all of them were—Therese could see clearly in the darkness. She could also sense everything around her, both living and nonliving, and was a bit wary of a group of jelly fish floating near the surface above her. But her keen senses didn't protect her from the enormous seaweed that sprang up from the ocean floor and wrapped itself around her legs. The other gods were similarly bound, struggling against the plants with their swords. Therese's legs burned where the weeds entangled her. She conjured her sword, but every time she sliced away a stem, another took its place. She quickened her pace, worried she'd hold up the others. Meg swam to her side, her blonde curls loosed from their knot and flowing around her face, and helped Therese get free, and then they maneuvered as fast as they could behind Than through the narrow entrance of a sea cave. After a few twists and turns, they resurfaced inside of an above-water cave filled with sheep.

Get out of the water, Tizzie warned. *And invisibility won't help us against the Cyclopes. But do dim yourselves.*

Over here, Alecto said. *Behind the sheep.*

Than crouched beside Therese in the dark cave between a crowd of sheep and the moist stone wall. His sisters huddled with them.

Are you okay? he asked Therese.

Therese nodded. She was wet, cold, and frightened and wanted to reach out and hold his hand but didn't want to risk rejection again.

Instead, she asked, *Why doesn't Polyphemus wash his eye here, in the cave? Why go all the way to the shore to do it?*

He's afraid he'll drop it, Tizzie replied, who crouched on the other side of Therese. *And he can't swim. It's safer on the beach, where the water is shallow and where the waves will bring it back to him if he drops it.*

He's the son of Poseidon and he can't swim? Therese asked.

None of the Cyclopes can swim, Alecto explained from behind Than. *That's how Zeus keeps them trapped on the island. They can't build anything either, so they can't sail away.*

Well, that didn't seem fair. She recalled the favorite line from Hades: "Life isn't fair, but death is." Therese found herself agreeing with that sentiment more and more.

Just then, the giant stood up from his bed and stretched his fat arms over his head with a loud wail.

I'd forgotten how big they are, Meg said. *And filthy.*

And ugly, Tizzie added.

Than told Therese, *Odysseus and his men were once imprisoned here years after the Trojan War. Odysseus tricked the Cyclops by saying his name was "No one."*

Why "No one"? Therese asked, vaguely recalling the story from high school.

Than explained, *So when Odysseus attacked, Polyphemus kept shouting, "No one is attacking me!" The other Cyclopes just ignored him and Odysseus got away.*

I thought he said "No man," Therese said, remembering the story more clearly now.

"One" is a better translation from the ancient Greek, Alecto replied.

"Alright, yer dirty mops!" Polyphemus shouted in a booming voice. "It's time to get moving!"

How rude, Meg said in a tone of condemnation.

Therese was reminded that Meg enjoyed punishing those with poor manners, and as frightened as Therese was crouched behind the sheep in the cave of a Cyclops, she smiled at the thought of Meg punishing Polyphemus for the poor treatment of his sheep. Then Therese looked about the cave and realized how vulnerable they were to exposure.

What will we do when all the sheep have gone? What if he sees us? Shouldn't we god travel out of here?

If we leave too quickly, he'll see us on the beach, Than said. *And we'll lose the element of surprise.*

*But if we leave too late...*Therese couldn't finish the thought. *Why can't we zip home and zip back?*

The timing has to be just right, Than said. *Plus, god travel will make us vulnerable to our enemy. Whoever that is.*

We have to wait until he's taken the eye out himself, Meg explained. *If we try to take the eye out of the socket while fighting him, we could damage the eye, and then we won't be able to save Mom and Athena.*

I've got it, Alecto said. *Grab hold of a sheep and crouch behind it as you walk out with it. Keep the sheep between you and the Cyclops.*

Why can't he sense us? Therese grabbed fistfuls of wool of the nearest sheep and spoke to him. *It's okay, little lamb. I'm here to help.* When it bleated an objection, she quickly pierced the hearts of the sheep each of them were using as shields, and the sheep became their docile friends.

Polyphemus can't sense us because his eye may be sharp but his brain is not, Than said.

How do I get this sheep to stop licking me? Alecto complained.

97

When they reached the mouth of the cave, the sun was bright and the air fresh, but the wind blew the goddesses' hair. This wasn't a problem for Alecto, whose red spiky hair was short, but it was for the other three. They feared the blond, red, and black would stand out in stark contrast to the white wool of the sheep they were using as shields.

Where is a hair band when you need one? Therese communicated.

She pierced more of the sheep and asked them to huddle around them to better protect them all from the giant.

"Come on yer muts!" Polyphemus bellowed when he noticed the sheep were clumping close to the cave. "Come on out. I'll be right back."

Polyphemus turned his fat body toward the shore and shuffled clumsily across the sand.

Let's go closer to the beach, sweetheart, Therese said kindly to the sheep.

A few steps from the shore, Polyphemus turned and saw he'd been followed. "What yer stupid muttons doing? Go wait for me!"

Don't mind him, lovelies. I'll protect you, Therese said to the sheep she'd pierced.

The other sheep obeyed Polyphemus and trotted toward the hills, but enough stayed behind to protect the gods from the view of the Cyclops.

"Aw, yer stupid lot," Polyphemus said to the ones who'd stayed behind. "Do what yer like, but just yer wait. I'll kick yer around to teach yer a lesson."

98

I won't let that happen, you poor little lambs! Therese said.

Polyphemus turned to the shore and plucked out his eye. Therese could see the big round orb, the size of a softball, in his hand as he knelt by the water's edge.

Now! The Furies said.

All five of them leapt toward the Cyclops. Than pinned the giant's free arm down as the Furies snatched the eye from the end of the other.

Polyphemus wailed a thunderous cry, which alarmed the neighboring Cyclopes. Therese could see them ambling toward the shore, scattering sheep.

"Let's get out of here!" Alecto shouted.

"Point the eye toward the sheep! Now!" Therese said.

As Meg held the eyeball toward the sheep, Therese pierced Polyphemus's heart with an arrow.

"Okay! Let's go!" Therese shouted.

Then all four gods leapt into the air just as the other Cyclopes reached the shoreline.

"We promise to return it to you!" Than called to Polyphemus below.

"Father!" Polyphemus cried in a wretched voice that reverberated across the sea.

The land and sea quaked and the sound of a far off train alarmed the gods. Before they could make their escape, a humpback whale leapt into the air and took Meg and the eye of the Cyclops into its humongous mouth.

Thinking quickly, Therese placed herself before the whale and shot it with her arrow.

"Release her, friend!" Therese commanded.

The whale lifted Meg, still holding the eye, out on its tongue long enough for Meg to shoot up into the sky.

Then a streak of lightning shot down from the clouds and struck Meg. The Fury dropped the eye and fell toward the sea.

***

Than saw the attack from Zeus coming, but he hadn't had time to warn Meg.

"Save Meg!" Than cried. "I'll get the eye!"

Than multiplied into the hundreds and swarmed around the one of him who caught and carried the eye. Lightning zapped at the outside layers of his swarm and grazed him a few times with painful surges of electrical fire. Every single one of him could feel the shocks that grazed him. Thankfully he suffered no direct hits, and he flew on, as low as he could without getting too close to the sea, where a school of sharks followed below him.

Do you have Meg? Than asked as he neared the chasm to the Underworld.

There was no reply.

***

Therese clutched Meg's foot as the other two Furies each grabbed an arm just before Meg was about to hit the surface of the sea. Before they could surge back up into the air, something giant lurched from the waves. A huge creature with slimy, marbled skin and a tube-like head emerged, flailing long tentacles that snatched at them. Meg was still unconscious, and before anyone could prevent it from happening, one of the long tentacles wrapped around her and took her under the sea.

Therese and the two other Furies dived after the creature, conjured their swords, and struck at the tentacles. Therese tried to shoot an arrow at the beast's heart, but the water shifted the arrow's path, and she was unsuccessful after three tries. Meanwhile, the creature sunk deeper and deeper into the abyss, taking them all with it.

***

When Than delivered the eye of Polyphemus to his father, his father had more bad news.

"The Malevolent has taken hostages—Hecate's familiars and the mortal Jen Holt."

"Jen? How…"

"You're running out of time," Cybele hissed in her manly voice. "Point the eye toward the stone goddesses and repeat after me."

Hades did as Cybele instructed.

"How do we know we can trust her?" Than asked, fearing for his mother's life.

"Silence, Than," Hades commanded. "You do not know all. Patience." Then to Cybele. "Proceed."

Cybele pronounced a string of words in ancient Greek, most of which Than recognized, but none of which he'd spoken for centuries. Hades repeated the words. Than interpreted them to mean, "Medusa's eyes did turn you cold and white as snow and hard as rock, but mine will now reverse her curse and what you were will turn you back."

The stone of the statues began to crack.

"They're crumbling! Stop this!" Hades cried.

"Mother! What's happening?" Than shouted.

As the bits of stone fell away, Athena and Persephone emerged, unscathed, from the rubble. Both of them gasped for air.

Than let go of the breath he'd been holding.

"Water," Persephone said.

Hades snapped his finger, and vessels of water appeared in each of the goddesses' hands.

"My dear Persie!" Hecate said with joy as she ran across the room and threw her arms around the Queen of the Underworld. "That's one less worry on my mind!"

"Thanatos," Hades said suddenly, handing the eye of Polyphemus over to him. "The Furies and Therese are in danger. Return to Cyclopes Island and parley the eye for the girls."

"I should take the chariot," Than said.

"Of course," Hades replied.

***

Therese felt the stinging suckers draw her blood to the surface of her skin, but she fought with her one free arm and sliced the tentacle in half. Once free, she swam toward the long, tubular head of the beast, slicing tentacles as they grabbed at her. The closer she got to the beast's eyes, the less able it was to reach her. Soon she realized that the head of the beast was the safest place to be—until it opened its gigantic mouth.

As she heard Tizzie scream in agony, Therese took an arrow from her quiver and dived, head first, through the creature's ring of teeth. Her foot narrowly escaped getting bit in half. The blood oozed around her, nearly suffocating her, until she remembered she could breathe underwater, so she could probably breathe in blood. She told herself to get a grip and think and to forget about the pumping membranes sucking her down. She plunged through the narrow membranes until she finally came upon the heart and pierced it with her arrow.

Get to the creature's eyes, Therese said to the Furies. *Whomever he looks upon will be able to get him to cooperate.*

Therese hoped either Tizzie or Alecto would manage to be seen by the beast, but, just in case they were not, she forced her way through the creature's innards and out the other side, taking with her a pool of blood. With the speed of light, she negotiated through the flailing tentacles, back toward the creature's face, met its terrifying eyes, and commanded, "Be still, my friend!"

Immediately, the creature relaxed its arms and hung limp in the sea. Alecto appeared beside her with Meg in her arms, but where was Tizzie?

***

Swift and Sure pulled Hades's chariot from the chasm and up into the bright morning with Than behind the reins. Like a flash, Than arrived at Cyclopes Island with the eye of Polyphemus in his hand.

Down below, he saw Polyphemus sitting with his sheep, petting them and sobbing from his eyeless socket.

At least he'll be nicer to his sheep, Than thought.

Hovering in the chariot just above the Cyclops, Than shouted, "Your eye for the Furies and the goddess of animal companions. We want safe passage away from this place."

"Father!" cried the Cyclops. His voice resounded across the sea.

***

Therese heard Than calling to her, but she was busy searching for Tizzie. She told Alecto to go on ahead of her and take Meg to the chariot. Therese could sense Tizzie near the bottom of the sea, and when she finally found her lying on a bed of anemone, she lifted the Fury in her arms and surged into the air.

***

Thanatos was relieved to see Therese and Tizzie join him and his other sisters in the chariot. He delivered the eye to Polyphemus by quietly laying the eye in the giant's lap ("What? I see me leg! What yer know, me lambs, but I've found me eye!"), and then Than turned the chariot back toward the Underworld.

"They aren't dying," Than said of Meg and Tizzie. "Only stunned. Apollo has agreed to meet us in Father's chambers."

104

Therese gave him a relieved smile, and although he returned it, his quickly turned into a frown.

"What is it?" Therese asked.

He hated to tell her bad news. He wished he could sweep her up in his arms and assure her that all would soon be well, but he wasn't so sure it *would* be. "Clifford and Jewels are safe, but Melinoe the Malevolent has taken Jen and Hecate's familiars as her prisoners."

Chapter Ten: The Prisoners

Upon the crest of the tallest mountain for miles in the blistery snow, Jen sat bound by leather straps at her wrists and ankles against the entrance to a cave, where she was forced to look at what the monster warned was a twenty-thousand-foot drop. The Doberman named Cubie and the weasel named Galin were also tied and lying in the snow on either side of her. The monster, half white and half black, stood over Jen and her fellow prisoners. Beside the monster were two ghosts invisible to Jen, one which was called Sisyphus and the other Medusa.

With nothing but a bearskin thrown over her, Jen was freezing, and she could barely breathe. Her teeth chattered, her body trembled, and her head spun from the high elevation.

The monster had brought Jen and the animals to this mountain cave and left them in the custody of the ghosts, which were ordered around by the monster. Maybe the ghosts weren't real. Jen couldn't see or hear them, except for an occasional howl that might have been the wind.

But now, after what must have been at least an hour, the monster had returned and was staring at her. The monster had a white eye on the black side of her strangely-shaped face and a black eye on the white side, and swollen red veins appeared around her nostrils and lips. Thin and tall, she had hairy moles all over and a hump on the white side of her body near her shoulder. Her black leg was thinner than the white, like an ostrich's leg.

"Who are you? What do you want from us?" Jen asked through her chattering teeth.

"What was a mortal doing in the Underworld?" the monster asked.

"I don't know," Jen said. "My friend, Hip, took me there to see my friend, Therese." Tears pricked the back of Jen's eyes. She wanted her mom and Pete and Bobby. She wanted to go home. "Please, let me go."

"Hypnos? Is that who you mean?" the monster asked in her stern and scratchy voice.

"I, I, I only know him as Hip."

"The god of sleep?"

Jen's mind whirled. God? "I think so, yes."

"You, Hecuba!" the monster kicked the Doberman. "What do you know of this?"

The dog winced. "Hypnos brought the mortal home to prove to her that he's a god."

"Is he in love with her?" the monster asked.

"I do not know," the dog replied.

The monster slapped Jen's face with a rough and bony claw. "Is he in love with you?"

Jen flinched and cupped her cheek. "We've only just met."

"You're worthless to me alive then." The monster rolled her eyes and sighed. "I suppose I'll have to kill you. I can use your ghost in my army."

The monster conjured up a sword and raised it over Jen. Jen squeezed her eyes shut and told her mother she loved her.

"Wait!" the weasel said. "This mortal is important to the goddess of animal companions."

Jen opened her eyes. She had no idea what the talking weasel meant.

"You speak of Therese, yes?" Melinoe asked. "I was promised her in the first place, not this girl."

"She's soon to marry Thanatos!" the dog added.

Jen bit her tongue. Blood flooded into her mouth. She wanted to spit, but didn't dare. Therese was a goddess?

The monster lowered her sword, and the weapon vanished. "Hmm. Maybe I'll put off the death of the mortal for now."

"She'll die in this cold," the weasel said. "Then she'll be no good to you. You should make a fire, to keep her alive and valuable. Thanatos will do anything to get her back."

"He wouldn't want a despondent bride," the dog added.

"Yes. A fire," the monster said. "Sisyphus! Collect some wood from below. Medusa! Gather kindling! And make it quick!"

"Who are you?" Jen asked again. "And what do you want?"

The monster turned and glared at Jen. "My name is Melinoe the Malevolent, and I want to rule the Underworld."

***

Therese looked at Than with disbelief as he lowered the chariot down from the bright sky toward the chasm that led to the Underworld. "Cubie, Galin, and, and, did you say Jen?"

"I'm sorry, Therese."

But that couldn't be, Therese thought. Her best friend in the clutches of the goddess of ghouls?

Than flew his father's chariot past Cerberus into the gates through the corridor leading to the garage. He parked and released Swift and Sure to the stables. Then he and Alecto carried Tizzie and Meg down the corridor along the Phlegethon as Therese followed dumbly behind.

She couldn't believe her best friend had been stolen by the Malevolent. It was mindboggling to even think of Jen down here in the Underworld to begin with, and now she was a prisoner of an insane tormentor. She shuddered as she imagined what Jen might be going through.

"Poor Jen," she whispered to herself as they neared Hades's chambers. "And poor Cubie and Galin. I've got to do something." Tears streamed from her eyes.

Therese was relieved to make telepathic contact with Clifford and Jewels, who were safe inside Hecate's rooms, and equally relieved to see Persephone and Athena fully recovered in chairs beside Hades, Apollo, and Hip. Cybele had not moved from her position on Hades's couch. Therese sensed a powerful spell binding Cybele to her seat. Hecate was also there, sitting at a round table in the back of the room, sobbing with her face in her hands. Therese crossed the room to Hecate's side.

Therese comforted Hecate while Apollo revived the two Furies. Meg and Tizzie were able to sit up, and after eating a handful of pomegranate seeds, were fully recovered.

"What kind of beast was that?" Tizzie asked. "I've never seen one before today."

"A giant squid," Hades replied. "No doubt sent by my dear brother, Poseidon."

"Perhaps he meant only to avenge the wrong we did to his son," Than suggested.

Therese loved the fact that Than looked for the good in everyone and assumed innocence until proven otherwise.

"Perhaps," Hades said. "But we should think on it more as we listen to what Cybele has to say."

Therese wondered how the prisoner figured into the drama unfolding before her. She'd not heard much about this goddess, except that she was sometimes prayed to by mortals when they wanted to have a family. She'd also heard that Cybele was born with both male and female parts and was somehow castrated and made decidedly female. Than once said Cybele was like Dionysus—a rebel god who lived on the fringe of the pantheon and had little to do with the rest of the immortal world.

The gods and goddesses moved their seats into a circle resembling the court at Mount Olympus. Therese guessed this was how groups of deities discussed things. All of the major gods of the Underworld were present except for the Fates and Charon. Athena and Apollo had remained, too. Therese hoped they would make saving Jen, Cubie, and Galin their top priority.

Hades said, "I've asked Athena and Apollo to stay and hear what Cybele has already told me. They have sworn on the River Styx that they were not involved in the recent strikes against us and have no more information than we do. Cybele?"

Cybele's curly black hair fell to her shoulders, and although her eyes and nose were soft and feminine, her chin, Adam's apple, and voice were manly, making her overall appearance to be that of a manly female. When she spoke, she looked around the room at everyone, and not just at the most powerful gods.

"The attack on the Underworld was a diversion," Cybele began.

"A diversion from what?" Athena asked.

"That was my question, too," Meg said.

"You," the manly goddess said, pointing at Athena.

Therese gasped. Why would someone strike the Underworld to get to Athena? That made no sense.

The Furies turned to one another with looks of confusion.

"What do you mean?" Athena asked. "What has it to do with me?"

"For centuries, you have asked Zeus to free your mother from his body," Cybele said. "He swallowed Metis while she was already pregnant with you, isn't that right?"

"He'd heard a prophecy," Athena said. "Metis would have a son who would overthrow Zeus as Zeus overthrew his father, Kronos."

"Inside Zeus's belly, your mother nurtured you and made your armor," Cybele said.

Therese furled her brow and wondered how that was possible. The gods amazed her more and more with their powers, and she had to constantly remind herself that she was one of them.

"I wear it every day. It reminds me of her. My memory is weak, though." Athena frowned. "I suppose Therese and Than have shown me that it's possible to stand up to Zeus for what you want, as long as you accept the consequences. I admire them for that."

Blood rushed to Therese's cheeks. The goddess of wisdom admired her? She shared a smile with Than, though looking at him only reminded her of the pain she had caused him.

"I want my mother here with me, but Zeus refuses to allow Hephaestus to break open his skull again."

"It's not the pain alone Zeus fears," Cybele said. "Your mother is believed by many to be the source of Zeus's wisdom. Without your mother inside his body, he might become an incompetent king."

Hades said, "Even if Zeus felt he could free Metis without freeing her son—your brother—he wouldn't do it because he wants your mother's wisdom for himself."

Therese frowned at the level of selfishness necessary to swallow a person whole and keep her inside of you so you could benefit from her wisdom.

"But every time I ask, he seems more open to the possibility," Athena said. "I'd begun to hope that soon…"

"He'll never agree," Cybele said. "And rather than face you and tell you the truth, he wanted you turned to stone."

Athena gasped. "Me? His favorite child?"

"Cybele speaks the truth," Apollo put in.

"Then why turn me to stone as well?" Persephone asked.

"You and Hestia were never meant to look upon Medusa," Cybele said. "And although Zeus reversed the curse on his beloved servant, Hestia, he kept you imprisoned in the stone, Lady Persephone, because he wanted to keep the gods of the Underworld distracted. He needed to appease Melinoe."

"The Malevolent?" Hip asked.

"But how?" Tizzie cried.

"Impossible!" Alecto snapped.

"How does Melinoe figure into Zeus's plans?" Persephone asked.

"Yes, do tell us," Hades said. "You and I had not gotten to this part yet, and I am anxious to know the answer to that question."

"Brace yourself," Cybele warned.

"I'm listening," Persephone said.

Therese gripped the arm of her chair with a sense of foreboding.

Cybele said, "Zeus is the real father of Melinoe."

"How can that be?" Hades roared, jumping from his seat and crossing to the center of the circle. He looked to Apollo.

"Cybele speaks no lie," Apollo said.

112

Therese flinched from the deafening roar of the voice of Hades. She wanted to cup her hands to her ears but feared making him angrier. Than and his siblings looked at one another in horror.

"I've never been unfaithful!" Persephone cried, also standing.

The King and Queen of the Underworld glared at one another in fear and horror.

"Persephone speaks the truth as well," Apollo said.

Athena gawked. "How can they both be telling the truth?"

"Zeus deceived Persephone," Cybele explained. "He disguised himself as you, Lord Hades."

Persephone lifted her hand to her mouth and closed her eyes. Hades took her into his arms and comforted her, wearing obvious relief on his face.

Therese was glad when the tension between Than's parents was dissolved. She could read the same on the faces of the others.

"How do you know this?" Apollo asked Cybele.

"Zeus told me. I was originally part of the plan to ruin the House of Hades."

Hades spun around and bellowed, "What did you say? You told me none of this before." The voice of the King of the Underworld thundered throughout the cavernous room.

"There was not time before, Lord Hades."

Therese sought Than's eyes, which were already trained on her. She wished he was beside her rather than across the room.

I'm frightened, she said to him.

I'm sorry about all of this, he replied.

I love you, Than. I've always loved you.

He closed his eyes.

I was afraid romantic love could not withstand immortality, she explained. *But Aphrodite helped me to see I was wrong. I'm so sorry.*

Than opened his eyes and lifted his head. *Are you saying you want to marry me?*

Yes. Therese gave him a subtle smile, and she saw the corners of his mouth twitch, too.

The voice of Hades interrupted their private exchange. "How does Zeus plan to ruin my house?"

"He doesn't," Cybele replied.

"No riddles, please," Athena said.

Cybele shook her head. "No riddle. Zeus never intended to bring down this house. He only wanted Melinoe to believe it. He wanted me to believe it, too. His attack was meant to create a diversion as he set Medusa and Sisyphus free. Zeus knew Medusa's first priority would be to reclaim her head from Athena's shield."

"So his only intention was to turn me into stone?" Athena asked.

Therese glanced back at Than. Hip and the Furies exchanged looks of shock as well. All of this to turn Athena to stone? But why?

"Only until he could give you my forgetting formula, which I told him would make you forget everything prior to your birth," Cybele said. "He planned to return you to your former state after anointing you with my potion."

Hades crossed the room and returned to his seat, as did Persephone beside him.

"She speaks the truth?" Hades asked of Apollo.

Apollo nodded. "I sense no deceit."

"So all Zeus wanted was to get Athena off his back about her mother?" Hades surmised.

Zeus had put them all in jeopardy to maintain his power, Therese thought. She wondered if that made him a good or a bad ruler. She supposed a good ruler needed to maintain control, but at what cost?

"Yes," Cybele said. "But there never was a forgetting potion. When Zeus came to me, asking me if I could produce one, I told him yes, so I could expose him to you and to Melinoe, who has been misused by Zeus for centuries."

Persephone stood up again. "Misused how?"

"After revealing himself as her father, he told her that Hades tried to kill her while she was in Persephone's womb."

Persephone's mouth fell open and Hades frowned.

"I would never do such a thing to my own child!" Hades said. "No wonder she despises me."

"But Zeus would," Cybele said. "When Zeus realized he'd made Persephone conceive a child, he tried to destroy it before it was fully formed, worried it would resemble him and betray his deed to you and to his queen."

Persephone put her face in her hands and began to weep.

"Persephone awoke before Zeus could carry out his plan," Cybele continued.

"Poor Melinoe!" Persephone cried. "My poor child! Deformed by her own father!"

"She may be poor, indeed, Lady Persephone," Cybele said, "but she believes her father Zeus to be in league with her against you, and at this very moment she plans to do everything in her power to bring down this house."

Therese shuddered.

"Zeus told her that Hades was responsible for her deformities," Cybele continued. "And he told me that Hades was responsible for mine."

"But that's not true!" Hades shouted.

"I know," Cybele assured him. "I found the truth for myself, which is why I could no longer help our lord. Just as Zeus was responsible for Melinoe's deformity, so, too, he was responsible for maiming me."

"But why?" Persephone asked.

"I can see his motivation for wanting to destroy Melinoe to protect himself," Hecate said. "But why did he harm you?"

"He was afraid that a god that was both male and female would be more powerful than he," Cybele replied. "So Zeus ordered Dionysus to choose a gender for me. The wine god's sensibilities were apparently too delicate for him to carry out the deed himself, so he waited until I was drunk from his wine and sound asleep. Then he tied a cord from my manly part to my ankle, so that when I got up..." Tears streamed down Cybele's cheeks.

Tears pricked Therese's eyes and a shiver worked its way down her spine. Poor Cybele. Zeus was a monster.

"I'm so sorry," Hecate said.

"That's terrible," Persephone added.

The other gods were silent for many minutes until Apollo broke it.

"What role does Sisyphus play in Zeus's scheme?"

"I only know that the ghosts of Sisyphus and Medusa were promised to Melinoe," Cybele said. "And I believe Zeus hopes to make her content with that in the end, once she sees he will not hand over the Underworld."

"But why my Cubie and my Galin?" Hecate asked.

"And Jen," Hip added.

"Melinoe believed she was getting Therese and perhaps Hecate. I'm sure she's furious at having kidnapped a mortal, whom she will see as utterly useless to her. She will likely kill the mortal girl and enslave her ghost as part of her army."

"No!" Therese cried.

"An unfortunate casualty, to be sure." Hades said. "I'm sorry, children."

"Unfortunate, indeed," Apollo said kindly.

Athena nodded with dismay.

"She will likely try to parley with Hecuba and Galin," Cybele said. "But I do not know her plans. Zeus did not speak in my presence of strategies beyond kidnapping Therese. And once Zeus learns I've conspired with you against him, whatever his plans were before will likely change."

At that moment, Therese grasped her locket near her throat and reached out to Melinoe. *Melinoe, wherever you are, I will come to you if you spare my friend. You can have me if you set her free.*

The scratchy voice of the Malevolent echoed in Therese's head. *Swear on the River Styx you will tell no one. Swear you'll come alone.*

I swear.

***

As angry as Than felt over the current threat to his father's house, he was filled with joy. He finally understood what was going on with Therese. She *hadn't* pushed him away because she had never loved him; she had done it because she had feared losing him. He understood why she would doubt the longevity of romantic love when faced with the many stories of the sexual escapades of the gods, especially those of Zeus. Than was grateful to Aphrodite, still his favorite aunt, for helping Therese to see that not all gods were so frivolous with their hearts.

He looked across his father's chamber at Therese and noticed the subtle smile she had shared with him moments ago turn into a frown. As Cybele and Hades predicted the likely death of Jen, Therese's face turned pale. Before Than could send her a reassuring prayer that he would do everything in his power to save the hostages, Therese vanished.

Everyone in the room noticed, and they turned their eyes to Than.

"She must have gone to find Jen," Than said.

"But how?" Hip asked. "Hecate and I searched everywhere."

"She's made a deal," Hades said.

Than knew his father spoke the truth, and his stomach formed a tight knot as helplessness and despair washed over him. "My father's right. She offered herself in exchange for Jen's freedom. That's the kind of person she is." Than crossed his arms at his chest and stood from his chair. His pulse quickened as he clenched his fists.

"Can you make contact with her?" Persephone asked.

"She won't reply," Than said, fighting the anger and despair. He wanted to punch something, to destroy something. For centuries he'd lived and never had he felt so much anger. *I'm losing it, Father.*

"Try the Malevolent," Hades offered.

"Nothing," Than said. "Can anyone get through to her? Mother?"

"She won't respond," Persephone said. "I've been telling her I didn't know about Zeus. I've told her how sorry I am. I even shared Cybele's information that Zeus never intended to give her the Underworld. But she won't answer me." Persephone covered her face with her hands and wept.

"I wish you would not have done so, Lady Persephone," Cybele said. "Now Zeus will know I've been talking to you."

"He would have suspected it by now regardless," Hades said. "Melinoe must have informed him by now, and if not, he suspected it once I sent my people to get the eye of the Cyclops."

"Zeus is no fool," Apollo agreed.

"And now his suspicions shall be confirmed when Melinoe questions him," Cybele said. "I would have bought you more time, but now I advise you to prepare your house for battle."

Than disintegrated and dispatched to his chambers where he released his anger and frustrations in a loud roar. Back in his father's sitting room, everyone heard the wail and looked at him with concern.

"I'm okay," he assured them.

"Whom can we trust?" Athena rose to her feet. "If my own father is behind this, I no longer know my friends from my enemies."

"Yes," Hades agreed and also stood. "And even though all but Zeus, Poseidon, and Hera said before Apollo that they were not behind the first attack on my house, that doesn't mean their help hasn't been solicited by our enemies since."

"We need to tread carefully," Than acknowledged. "But we need to find out who is on our side."

"How do we do that?" Alecto asked. "Without making ourselves vulnerable to more treachery?"

As the others discussed ways to discover their true allies, Than continued to reach out to Therese, to no avail. He had to find a way to save her from the clutches of the Malevolent. He sent a prayer to Hip.

We've got to find them, Than prayed. *And I have an idea.*

Chapter Eleven: Lost

As soon as Therese appeared before the Malevolent in the cave at the uppermost peak of the Himalayas, she was immediately bound by a powerful spell that knocked her to the icy ground. Although her arms and ankles were bound in leather, the straps were reinforced by magic beyond Therese's experience. She did not have the strength to free herself.

She studied the ghosts that flanked Melinoe. Sisyphus she'd seen before, but she'd never really looked at Medusa. Although the physical head of Medusa would turn anyone who looked upon it to stone, the soul itself had no such power, and Therese couldn't stop herself from staring at the dozen transparent snakes hissing above the Gorgon's striking face, like Tizzie's whenever she turned into the avenger of murder.

However frightening the soul of Medusa appeared, it was nothing compared to the malformed face and body of the Malevolent. If the monster weren't as cruel as she was ugly, Therese might feel sorry for her.

Jen huddled, shivering against the cave wall between Cubie and Galin. A pathetic, scraggily fire cast flames the size of dimes between Jen and the animals on one side of the cave and Therese on the other. Between the mouth of the cave and the fire stood Melinoe and her ghosts.

"Send the mortal home," Therese demanded without saying anything to Jen. She didn't want Melinoe to know how much she loved her best friend, because then the monster might use that love against Therese.

"That wasn't part of our bargain," the Malevolent sneered.

Therese glanced at the souls of Sisyphus and Medusa chuckling beside their mistress, who obviously had them under her control. Therese wondered how long it would take for the two souls to realize their own captivity. Had Melinoe made promises to them?

"Me for the mortal. That was the deal."

"I didn't swear I'd send her home," Melinoe said cheerfully. "I swore I'd set her free." She turned to Sisyphus. "Cut the mortal loose."

Sisyphus took a sharp rock from behind him and cut the leather straps at Jen's arms.

"Aren't you tired of dealing with rocks?" Therese asked Sisyphus. "How is taking orders from Melinoe any better?"

The ghost of Sisyphus paused, as if to consider Therese's question.

"Enough!" Melinoe snapped. "Cut the mortal loose."

Sisyphus obeyed. Jen shivered and staggered as she climbed to her feet.

Therese glared at the Malevolent. "She'll die out there!"

"Exactly," Melinoe said. "And then I'll draft her into my army." The Malevolent laughed a blood-curdling shriek that made Medusa and Sisyphus howl.

Other howls came from the furthest recesses of the cave, and Therese sensed some of the Malevolent's army of ghouls dwelled there.

Jen looked at Therese with fear and unwittingly prayed, "What should I do?"

Jen wouldn't hear Therese if she prayed back, so she distracted Melinoe as long as possible, so Jen could remain near the warmth of the fire in the center of the cave. "What did humans ever do to you? Why do you torment them with your evil spirits? It's Zeus you should despise!"

"Silence!" Melinoe demanded.

"Hades loved you as his own!" Therese continued. "He would never harm you! Zeus was the one afraid of getting caught by Hera. He was the one who turned you into what you are in order to protect himself!"

"I said silence!" Melinoe shrieked.

"Think about it, Melinoe!" Therese insisted. "Why would Hades want to harm his own daughter? You could have been an ally and a help to him in his kingdom. Zeus, however, would have a motive for wanting to destroy you, to cover up his infidelity. To keep it all from Hera!"

Melinoe stood over Therese, bent her ugly face so that it was inches from Therese's face, and hissed, "I said silence!"

"You can't silence me!"

"Oh?" Melino levitated Galin over the cliff edge. "I said I'd set the mortal free, but I can do plenty of harm to Hecate's familiars."

Galin stared at Therese in terror. Cubie struggled with the leather straps binding her, suddenly mad with fear for her friend.

Therese clamped her quivering lips shut and said nothing. Tears formed in her eyes. How could she be so defenseless, so powerless to help?

Jen reached out with both hands toward the weasel. "She's going to fall! Please bring her back inside!" She stepped dangerously close to the cliff edge.

"Jen, no!" Therese cringed in horror as Jen slipped on the icy ground down the mountain slope and out of sight.

"Jen!" Therese cried. "Oh my god, no!"

Melinoe laughed as she returned Galin on the icy ground beside Cubie. Therese lowered her head into her hands and wept. She didn't care what Melinoe thought of her. Although Than would surely sense Jen's death and discover Melinoe's lair, Therese didn't care about rescue because her very best friend was gone.

***

Hip met Than in the field of poppies and clasped his brother's shoulder. There was something weighing on his mind. The war about to break between brothers had unsettled him.

"Than, listen to me."

"I'm listening."

"I'm sorry I brought Jen down here and put Therese in jeopardy," Hip said solemnly. "Say you forgive me."

Than gave Hip a half smile. "You couldn't know this would happen. You owe me no apology."

"Say you forgive me anyway."

"I forgive you." Than gave him a look of bewilderment.

"Thank you." Hip moved closer to his brother. "I don't ever want us to become like our father and his brothers: one brother attacking another—I just don't get it."

Than crossed his chest and covered Hip's hand with his own on his shoulder. "You have nothing to fear from me."

"I tease you all the time, bro. It's my greatest pleasure in life." Hip winked. "But before we carry out your plan, I want you to know that, whatever happens, you've always been the most important person in my life."

Hip had never seen his brother look so surprised, except for the day Therese first came flying into Than's arms.

"Is that really such a shock to you, bro?" Hip asked with a laugh.

"It's not a shock that you feel it," Than said. "Just that you'd say it. I think your time with the mortal has changed you."

Hip shrugged, and awkwardly stepped away, but what his brother said was true. There was something about this girl that made him long for a relationship outside of the world of dreams. He refused to think about that, though. Besides, maybe he was just riled and not thinking clearly. "Ready to get this show on the road?"

"Is she asleep then?" Than asked.

"Yeah, I sense it. I wish I could tell you where, but I can't, and I don't know how long we have."

Than laid down in the poppies and went to sleep. Soon, he entered the Dreamworld, where Hip led him through a series of strange dreams full of psychedelic colors, street fights, an enormous snake, and talking trees, until they came upon the one they were seeking. Jen hung from a tree branch in the middle of an empty meadow.

"The branch is about to break," she said as Hip and Than approached. "Will you catch me?"

Hip flew to her and gathered her up with one arm beneath her shoulders and another beneath her knees. It felt good to be close to her again, even in the world of dreams.

"How's this?"

She gave him a smile. "Good." Then she looked up into the tree. "But I think there are three others stuck up there. Can you save them, too?"

Hip carried Jen down to where fallen leaves had turned brown and had covered the ground. A wind blew the leaves, and the branches of the one tree in the middle of Jen's meadow swayed.

"Than?" Jen asked when Hip set her on her feet. Her teeth chattered. "Where's Therese?"

"Listen to me, Jen," Hip interrupted. "You were captured by the Malevolent. Cubie and Galin were with you."

"And Therese may be there, too," Than added.

"Can you remember?" Hip asked gently. He moved her blonde hair from her eyes and looked down at her. She was so lovely. Why did this mortal move him so deeply?

"The tree," she said. "They're up in that tree."

"And where is the tree?" Hip asked, caressing her cheek. "Did Melinoe the Malevolent take you to a forest?"

"Melinoe the Malevolent?" Jen pinched her brows together.

"She's half black and half white," Than said. "She has a hunchback and is covered in hairy moles."

"One of her legs is thinner than the other," Hip said. "And she may have Medusa with her."

The landscape changed into a snowy embankment, and jagged blades of ice shot up around them.

"I'm freezing," Jen said through her chattering teeth. "I can't move."

"Where are you?" Than asked desperately. He moved nearer to Jen's trembling projection only to stop abruptly. He gave Hip a look of concern. "She's dying."

Hip stiffened. He felt his tongue go numb and he could barely speak when he said, "What can we do?"

Than shook his head. "I wish I knew."

Hip put his arms around the shivering projection of Jen and used his power to warm her. "I don't know if this will work. Maybe if she's hot in her dream, her body will react. I just don't know."

Hip transformed the snowy embankment into a sandy desert with the sun blaring down on them. Sweat rose to the top of his skin as he conjured as much heat as he could muster.

"Help me, bro," Hip said.

Than moved beside them and wrapped his arms around Jen from the back. Hip gave his brother a grateful nod. Together they warmed Jen's psyche, hoping that maybe a fraction of that heat might intercept her death.

Then, without warning, she vanished.

***

Jen opened her eyes and found herself covered in a thick layer of snow on a thin ledge of the mountainside. The falling snow made it difficult for her to see how far down she had fallen from the cave where the monster had taken her prisoner. She turned her head and searched for the ground over the cliff edge and could just make out the slope of the mountain, the ground nowhere in sight and probably still thousands of feet below.

She sat up, dusting away the snow, and leaned her back against the mountainside, her knees bent, and her arms around her shins so that she formed a ball. Her body shook so violently from the freezing cold that she feared she might cause an avalanche. She looked up again at the snow above her, and, feeling hopeless, began to cry, but her tears turned to ice. She closed her eyes, wiped away the ice, and tried to think.

How did she get here? She'd been talking to Hip, and he'd told her the most outrageous thing she'd ever heard—that he was a god. He'd taken her to a warm cave—not by plane or bus or car. They'd been standing in front of Lemon Reservoir one minute, and then, the next, she felt like her guts were getting squeezed out of her, and then she was in a cave with crazy talking animals. Therese and Hip had left her with the talking animals and the monster had appeared. Clifford had barked up a storm, annoying the monster and escaping her clutches.

Jen shook her head. This had to be a dream. It had to be. Her mind couldn't accept the possibility that these extraordinary events were real.

Wait a minute. Dream. She'd just been dreaming of Hip. Had he been the *real* Hip, the supposed god of sleep, or just a part of her dream? Maybe if she closed her eyes, she could find out.

With chattering teeth, she whispered, "Hip."

Behind her lids, she saw white streaks, but she was still awake. Slowing down her breathing, she willed herself to relax. Where had she been in her previous dream? She'd been so warm. Oh, God, she missed that warmth. She pulled her feet closer to her body and tried to recall the source of the heat. The white streaks behind her eyes became huge hills of sand. A bright sandy desert! Yes, she could remember now. The sun shone down with unrelenting heat. Turning her face up to the sun, she took a deep breath, sank into the comforting heat, and…slipped down a hill on her bottom.

She flinched as she hit the ground.

"Jen!" Hip cried. "You're back!"

He ran up to her and helped her to her feet. Than came up beside them.

"Did you notice anything about your surroundings while you were awake?" Than asked.

Hip wrapped his arms around her from the front, and Than did the same from the back. She was sandwiched between two gods who were hot in more ways than one. Sweat dripped down their skin as the sun embroiled them and the sand reflected heat up into her eyes.

"Were you in a forest with trees?" Hip asked.

"Huh?" Jen met his beautiful blue eyes. His blond hair swept across his forehead, dripping in sweat.

"This feels so good," she purred, burying her face against his hot chest.

"Jen," Than said, lifting her head from behind. "Try to remember where you were before you fell asleep. Were you in snow?"

The desert instantly changed into a snowy embankment, and Jen shivered uncontrollably. "I'm on a mountainside," she said between chattering teeth. "I don't know where."

"Bring back the desert," Than said. "She's slipping from us again."

Hip conjured the desert landscape and the blaring sun, and Jen sank against him once again, but Than took a step away from them. "I have to go."

Jen wished Than would stay. The heat from his body was comforting, and now wind blew against her back.

"Don't!" Hip said too close to her ear.

"I have to, Hypnos. I can't disintegrate and do my duties while I'm here, and I think I have a better chance to save her if I go."

"Don't leave me, bro."

"I'll make this quick," Than said. "I promise."

Jen flinched when Than disappeared, and when she sought Hip's eyes, she saw fear in them.

***

Than disintegrated and returned to his duties, which he'd abandoned for the Dreamworld, and dispatched to the ruins of the Parthenon in Athens. Fortunately, it was dark and only a few of the tourists remained in the area. Invisible to them, Than stood beside Athena's statue and summoned her. She appeared minutes later in his father's chariot.

"God travel is dangerous for me right now," she explained. "I assume this is important?"

"I'm hunting the Malevolent," Than replied. "Hip and I spoke to her prisoner in the Dreamworld, and we believe Melinoe is camped on a mountain, but we don't know which one. If we could capture her, she could reveal the identity of our enemies."

"You've come to ask Amphisbaena?"

"Exactly, with your help. I don't have time to fight with her again."

Together they rode behind Swift and Sure to the west of the acropolis and parked near the entrance to Athena's sacred caves.

Chapter Twelve: Parsing Words

Therese's tears continued to stream down her face as she thought about poor Mrs. Holt and Pete and Bobby. How would she explain to them? It would be impossible. The thought of Jen dead made her regret everything. As much as she loved Than, she hated that her relationship had meant the death of her friend.

"Hey you!" The Malevolent kicked Therese on the thigh, but she didn't care, and it didn't hurt. The action was meant to humiliate, not injure.

Therese refused to meet the monster's eyes.

"Fine. I'm leaving to wrench the soul of the mortal from her body before I lose it to Thanatos." Then Melinoe added, "Sisyphus, you stay here. Medusa, come with me to hunt."

"Please!" Therese begged. "I'll do anything for you if you spare my friend!"

"You already will do anything for me," the Malevolent said with a laugh. "You'll see."

The monster and the ghost of Medusa flew from the cave and into the snow.

"I'm so sorry about your friend," Cubie said. "I wish I could have protected her."

"This isn't your fault," Therese said. "Melinoe tricked me. She said she'd free Jen, not see her safely home. Why didn't I see that coming?"

"Because you're not evil," Galin said. "You're heart's too pure to predict such treachery."

Sisyphus chuckled. "Because you're not as clever, that's why." He pointed to his head. "It takes cunning to get around a sworn oath."

Therese thought back to what the Malevolent had said: *Swear on the River Styx you will tell no one. Swear you'll come alone.*

I swear, Therese had said.

She clenched her jaw in frustration. If she told anyone where she was, she would be subjected to the Maenads for all eternity and no longer trusted among the other gods. It had taken Than the course of two years to regain the trust of Zeus, and some still looked down upon Than for breaking his oath. Should she follow in Than's footsteps to save Jen's soul from the Malevolent?

On the other hand, if Cybele were telling the truth (and Apollo says she was), and Zeus was behind Melinoe and the attack on the Underworld, how could his system of justice continue to rule the gods? Could Zeus still be the enforcer of sworn oaths when he himself had acted atrociously? Hadn't his recent involvement against Athena and the House of Hades rendered his authority questionable? Maybe Therese could make an argument in her defense. She could say the oath was sworn during a time of chaos and uncertainty and under extreme duress.

But hadn't that been true of nearly every oath ever sworn?

Uhh! She was wasting valuable time with all this pondering. She needed to act! Jen's soul could already be, at this very instant, enslaved by the monster.

Her oath to Melinoe played through her mind once more:

Swear on the River Styx you will tell no one. Swear you'll come alone.

I swear.

She had sworn she would tell no one. Then an idea struck her. Odysseus once went by the name of "No one" to trick the Cyclops, Polyphemus. When Polyphemus had cried, "No one is attacking me!" the other Cyclopes had ignored him.

Could Therese communicate with Odysseus?

***

Than and Athena entered Amphisbaena's cave in the underbelly of the acropolis, accosted by the dank smell of stagnant water and rot. They crossed the rocky cavern floor with caution, Than on one side of the thin ribbon of water dividing the cave in half, and Athena on the other. Athena called out to her two-headed serpent dragon, who was hiding, and asked for her favor.

"My life is in peril," Athena said.

"And so is the soul of your mother," Than added.

One of the two heads emerged from a high shelf at the back of the cave. The head was made of shiny blue scales and was crowned with bright red spikes down the center. Intense black eyes peered from two slits above a short snout and a darting, forked tongue.

"We need to know the location of the Malevolent," Athena asked.

"And your mother's soul," Than said again. "They're on a mountain, but we don't know which."

The second head emerged alongside the first, and a great hissing sound echoed inside the cave. A thick flame alighted across the top of the cavern, and the residue of smoke lingering behind spelled, "One says Ozarks. Two says Himalayas."

"Can you be more specific?" Athena asked. "Can you give us the name of a mountain?"

Another billow of fire illuminated the top of the cavern, and when the majority of the smoke cleared, the same words lingered in the air. "One says Ozarks. Two says Himalayas."

Than turned to Athena. "Two is the reliable one, in my experience, but I'll go at once to both."

He planned to disintegrate into the thousands to comb every square foot of both mountain ranges, but as he and Athena turned their backs on Amphisbaena, something monstrous shot up from the stagnant water between them and wrapped itself around the goddess of wisdom.

It was Poseidon with his golden net.

***

Hip clung to Jen's fragile, quivering projection beneath his illusion of the desert sun, feeling helpless and terrified. He'd never cared so much for a mortal's life as he found himself caring for this one. Why? Why did he care?

He supposed she first caught his attention the way she bravely endured the nightmares caused by her father's mistreatment of her. Despite the horrors of the night, she lived her life fully during the day. She worked hard on her mother's ranch, knew how to handle a horse, played the French horn admirably, swam with grace and speed, graduated in the top half of her high school class, and was a good friend to Therese. She didn't let her father's atrocious behavior stop her from living a normal teenager's life.

The most compelling reason he cared for this mortal was the chemistry between them—and that he couldn't explain. When he was around her, he was happiest, and that was all there was to it.

And now, he would lose her unless he could keep her from freezing to death. The cold winds must be taking their toll on her physical body, because her projection shivered violently in his arms.

Aeolus, that wind bag! Maybe he could help! Hip prayed to the god of gales.

Hypnos?

I'm in the world of dreams and am desperate for your help, Hip prayed.

You'll owe me one.

Obviously, cousin.

What would you have me do?

Can you trap the cold winds of every mountain range for an hour or so?

That's a mighty big request, cousin.

I'll owe you a mighty big favor.

Next he called on Chione, the snow nymph and wife of Boreas, the north wind, to allow the snowcapped mountains to melt. He asked Helios, the sun god, to speed up the process. All was going according to plan—Hypnos could feel Jen's trembling subside and the color return to her projection. This gave him hope that she'd be saved.

She raised her chin and looked up at him through her pretty blond lashes. "Why aren't you kissing me?"

He gave her a lascivious grin and put his mouth to hers.

Then, to his dismay, she disappeared.

***

Jen awoke on the wet, slick mountainside beneath a cheerful sun. The wind and snow had finally stopped blowing. She uncurled herself and looked around, both up toward the top from where she had fallen, and down below toward the ground she still could not see thousands of miles away.

Suddenly the monster appeared overhead shrieking with rage. "There you are, you little rodent! Now that the snow is melting, I can see you more clearly. How is it you're still alive?"

Jen didn't answer, but instead, climbed to her feet and pressed her back into the wet rock behind her. She grabbed a handful of loose stones. Her heart felt like it might explode.

The monster laughed. "What a good idea! Throw rocks at the goddess of ghosts and slip and break your neck! That would be perfect!"

"You promised to let me go!" Jen shouted. "If you take me, dead or alive, you'll break your word. Therese said you swore an oath to set me free."

"And that I did!" The monster said. "Are you not free?"

Jen backed up, seeking foot holds in the mountainside. "Get away from me!"

The monster swooped in close with a blood-curdling shriek, startling Jen, making her flinch. She lost her footing and dropped in a free fall through the chilly air.

Chapter Thirteen: Free Fall

Than scoured the mountain ranges of both the Ozarks of the United States and the Himalayas of the Far East. He was in constant fear that he would sense the death of Jen's soul before he would see her living body. He hoped for his brother and Therese's sakes that he would find the mortal in time.

As he combed every square foot of every mountain—disintegrating in the hundreds of thousands—he also flew home to report what had happened to Athena, confirming his father's suspicions that both of his brothers were in league against him.

"I tried to follow them," Than said, "But I lost them, and the waters around Poseidon's palace are heavily guarded by sea monsters."

In his conversation with his father and the other gods convened there, he paused when hundreds of thousands of miles away near the peak of Mount Everest, he spotted Jen falling through the thin air. He raced against time as she plummeted toward a nearby mountain, and he caught her just before she hit rock. Aware that her life was in danger the longer he held her, he took a chance and god traveled with her back to her home in Colorado, where he sat her on her bed and promised her she'd be safe. Melinoe the Malevolent had no use for one of the living—at least he hoped not.

"But what's going on?" Jen asked as he stepped away from her.

"Therese will explain everything later. I've got to go before my presence kills you."

Once Than had discovered Jen, he'd abandoned his search of the Ozarks to focus on Mount Everest, and it didn't take him long to find Therese bound by a powerful spell at the feet of Sisyphus. Before he could rush in to save her and Hecate's familiars, a bolt of lightning shot from the sky and struck him down. He couldn't move. All went dark, and he lost consciousness.

***

Therese watched in horror as Than fell through the air like a damaged airplane.

"I've got to do something!" she cried to Cubie and Galin. "Oh my god! That was Zeus's thunderbolt!"

"Zeus?" Galin cried in a feeble voice.

"Oh, no," Cubie said. "Zeus is behind this madness."

Sisyphus laughed at them.

Therese wondered if the duties of death would be transferred to her, as they were the time Than had been bitten by Ladon while she'd been holding up the sky in place of Atlas. On the one hand, she hoped so, because then, depending on the magic that bound her, she might be able to disintegrate and save herself and her friends from Melinoe. But on the other hand, she dreaded it, because she couldn't bear what it might mean for Than. The fact that he was immortal didn't assuage her fear of the injuries and debilitation he might have to endure for the rest of eternity.

If she were allowed to pray to any god without breaking her oath, she would. She thought again about trying to contact Odysseus. Would her argument that he was "No one," stand up in court? And even if she did contact him, what could he do about it? He was just another soul in the Underworld in the Elysian Fields. He had no memories and no free will. But maybe…maybe he was capable of taking orders from a god. Oh, she had to try something. She couldn't just sit here and do nothing.

She closed her eyes and reached out to Odysseus, but before she could make contact, Melinoe the Malevolent flew into the cave, with Medusa behind her, and screeched, "We're moving! Now!"

Zeus's chariot appeared near the cave entrance with Hera behind the reins. Therese, Galin, and Cubie were shoved into the back of it. Melinoe stood beside Hera, and the two ghosts flew behind as they passed the Himalayas toward the west and traveled across the Middle East and down toward the Mediterranean Sea to the island of Crete. Therese huddled beside Cubie and Galin, exchanging terrified looks as the wind, and in some places rain, blew against them. The chariot circled the highest mountain peak, and then Therese's stomach lurched as the chariot took a nose dive several thousand feet before coming to an abrupt halt outside of a dark cave.

"Keep them in there," Hera commanded.

Sisyphus grabbed Therese, Medusa grabbed Galin, and Melinoe grabbed Cubie. As soon as they were out of the chariot, Hera commanded her black stallions, and like a flame of fire, the chariot danced across the sky and away.

Melinoe and the ghosts carried the three prisoners into the dark cave. Therese could see perfectly with her goddess vision. The cave was large and round, and in the center was a pool of water where two nymphs sat soaking their feet. A goat stood near them chewing on a stick. As Sisyphus carried Therese further into the cave, she noticed another figure lying between the nymphs. One nymph was petting it and "Ooohing" and "aweing" over it, saying, "So beautiful. So lovely. I had no idea." At first, Therese thought it was another animal, but the closer she got, the more familiar the form appeared. Sisyphus dropped Therese in a heap across the pool from the nymphs, and once she recovered and sat up, she recognized the figure. It was Than!

She reached out to him with prayer, but received no response. He lay there, unmoving, as if dead.

"Is he alive?" Therese asked.

"She speaks to us?" one nymph said to the other.

Melinoe slapped Therese across the face. "Don't talk to them."

"What are you going to do with him?" Therese asked. "And us?"

"That's for me to know and for you to find out," Melinoe snapped.

Then she and her two ghosts flew away leaving Therese and her animal companions, and the still body of Than, alone with the nymphs and their goat.

***

Hip found himself being sucked from the Dreamworld as the dying souls around the world called to him. This could only mean one thing—both Therese and his brother were incapacitated. That was the only way the duties of the dead would fall on him. He disintegrated and dispatched to the souls beckoning him, and he went to his parents as well.

Only Hades, Persephone, Hecate, and Cybele remained in the chambers where the gods had convened earlier to discuss the attacks on the Underworld and the abduction of Athena. Hip's parents were outraged when Hip notified them of the transfer of duties and its implications.

"We have to find Thanatos," Hades said. "I've asked Apollo and the Furies to solicit aid from the Old Man of the Sea and his monstrous progeny in an effort to rescue Athena from Poseidon. But I will order the Furies to abandon that mission and leave Apollo to it, so your sisters can help you search for Thanatos."

"I can help both Apollo and the Furies," Hip suggested.

"Good idea," Hades agreed.

At that moment, Hip heard a prayer from Jen from her home in Colorado. His heart filled with joy, and he conveyed the news of her safety to his parents.

"Does she know anything of Cubie , Galin, and Therese?" Hecate asked, springing up from her chair.

Hip promised he would go to Jen and speak with her, though in his present role, he would not be able to stay too long lest he kill her. Privately, he couldn't wait to see her face again and to see for himself that she was safe.

Chapter Fourteen: Ida's Cave

Therese watched in despair as the two nymphs fondled Than's motionless body in the dank cave on the island of Crete. In between kisses and caresses, they cooed, "So beautiful. So yummy." Therese felt sick to her stomach. She was helpless to save him from their abuse. Therese's anger surged inside her along with the nausea.

She tried to distract the nymphs with her questions. "Why are we here? What is this place? Who are you?"

"Pay no attention to her, Ida," one nymph said to the other. "We aren't to speak with the prisoners."

"What cave is this?" Therese asked again, undeterred.

"It's a loathsome place," Galin joined in.

"Watch your words!" the one called Ida said.

"I agree, Galin," Therese said, glad to see something had finally riled the fondlers. "There's a stench here. It smells like dead fish and bad gas."

"And bad breath," Cubie added, catching on.

"Mind yourself!" the other nymph said. "You are speaking of King Zeus's childhood home!"

"That doesn't make it smell any nicer!" Therese taunted.

"Why would the lord of the gods grow up in a place like this?" Cubie said. "So unworthy."

"His mother gave him to us when he was a baby," Ida said.

"Kronos was going to swallow him, like he did the rest of his children, to prevent the prophecy from coming true," the other nymph added.

"We saved Zeus's life and helped him to grow strong," Ida said.

"If it weren't for us, none of the Olympians would be alive, much less in power!" the second declared.

"So watch what you say to us and show more respect!"

The goat bleated its excitement.

As the nymphs scolded Therese and her animal companions for their irreverence, Therese reached out to Odysseus, and was utterly amazed when he replied.

***

Before Hip left his parents, another surprise came to him while he was escorting souls to the Elysian Fields. Odysseus approached him and said, with a blank look on his face, "The goddess of animal companions has commanded me to speak with you."

In his father's chambers, Hypnos turned to his parents. "Wait! I have a message!"

Back in the Fields of Elysium, he put his hand on the shoulder of old Odysseus and asked, "What does she say?"

Odysseus bowed and said, "She and Thanatos, along with Hecate's familiars, have been taken to a cave beneath the highest mountain on the island of Crete."

Hypnos thanked the old demigod and again, turned to his parents with a joyous grin. "I know where Thanatos is!"

Cybele smiled when Hip conveyed the news from Odysseus.

"Metis must have withdrawn from counseling Zeus," Cybele said. "Perhaps, even in his belly, she's aware of Athena's abduction."

"What leads you to this conclusion?" Hades asked.

"Zeus has imprisoned Thanatos and the others in his infant home, forgetting about the close proximity of my Curetes," Cybele explained.

"I'm not familiar with your Curetes," Hip said.

"My dancing warriors," Cybele replied. "When Rhea hid Zeus in the cave of Mount Ida, my Curetes crashed their shields together to drown out the sound of Zeus's cries, so Kronos would suspect nothing. The Curetes live near that mountain still."

"Can they help us?" Persephone leaned toward Cybele with a hopeful expression.

"Of course," Cybele replied. "But first, we need a plan."

***

Jen's mother came to check on Jen once more before turning in for the night.

"You sure you're okay, baby girl?" her mother asked. "You still look as white as a ghost."

Her mother's choice of words sent a shiver down Jen's spine. "I'll be alright. I just need some rest." She felt chilled from her time in the snowy mountains.

"I wish I would have known you were up here all this time. I was worried sick. Thought you'd gone off with Hip."

"I'm sorry. I did go for a walk with him, but then I started feeling worse, so I came up to bed," Jen lied. She couldn't very well tell her the truth.

"I hope you feel better, baby girl."

"Thanks, mom."

"Good night then." Her mother leaned over and kissed Jen's forehead. "Sweet dreams."

When her bedroom door clicked shut, Jen closed her eyes, hoping to find Hip. She couldn't believe all that had happened that day—being told Hip was a god, being taken to his Underworld home, then being kidnapped by a grotesque and evil monster, freezing in a mountain cave, and then almost plummeting to her death. Than had caught her just as she was about to hit the ground and long after she had peed in her pants. A hot shower still hadn't warmed her back up after so many hours in the snow. Nor did she feel confident that she hadn't lost her mind. Maybe none of it was real and she'd finally gone off the deep end after years of trying to hold it all together.

"Please, Hip," she whispered.

"Don't freak out," a voice came close beside her.

She opened her eyes in a flash and lay still, like a statue.

"It's me, Hip."

She sat up so fast, she made her head hurt. Both hands rushed to her skull and held it until the spinning stopped.

"Are you okay?" He took several steps back.

"No. What the heck happened today? I'm so confused! Is Therese okay?"

"I can't stay long," he said. "I've taken my brother's place as the god of death, and my presence is a danger to you. I just wanted to tell you…I'm sorry I got you mixed up in my problems."

"You can't stay?" She hadn't heard much except that he had to go.

"I'll be back as soon as I can. But can you tell me if Cubie and Galin are still with the Malevolent?"

"Yes. She's got them tied up. And Therese, too. What's she going to do with them?"

"Let me worry about that." He moved closer and gave her a quick kiss before backing to the edge of the room.

Jen felt herself growing weak and short of breath.

"I'll be back," Hip said just before he vanished.

***

Therese was shocked when shortly after the two nymphs had lectured her about the sacredness of their dank cave, a man with a bee hive in his hands and a swarm of bees around his armored head entered the cave and addressed them angrily. He wore armor on his chest but nothing more than a loin cloth on the lower half of his body, as if he'd forgotten to finish dressing.

"Ida and Andrasteia!" the man roared.

"Father?" they replied in unison.

"Come with me, now!" he shouted, his voice echoing throughout the cave.

A single bat fluttered past Therese and flew into the light.

"But the prisoners!" the one called Andrasteia objected.

"They are not your concern!" he commanded. "You're in danger here. Now, come!"

"What of our goat?" Ida asked.

"Leave her and come!" he said before he vanished.

The two nymphs gave Therese a suspicious glare and then disappeared.

"I wonder what that was about," Cubie said when she was left alone with her fellow captives.

"I wish I knew." Therese lay on her side and rolled across the dirty cavern floor, around the edge of the pool, and to the back side of the cave where Than lay motionless near the water. Dragging herself by the elbows, she maneuvered herself to his side and put her face near his.

"Than? Can you hear me?"

She longed to touch him, but her wrists and ankles remained bound, and the leather straps were unyielding.

"Is he breathing?" Galin asked.

"I can't tell," Therese replied. "I think I see a slight movement in his chest, but it could be my own wishful thinking. Oh, Than!"

Squirming and scooting into position, she put her head against his chest and listened. "I hear a heartbeat! It's faint, but there!"

"Thank goodness," Cubie said.

"Keep trying to wake him," Galin suggested.

"I will," Therese said. "Can you reach out to Hecate and tell her where we are? I swore an oath to tell no one, but maybe you can."

"I've been trying," Galin said. "But the Malevolent made us drink something when she first captured us, and I think it was a blocking potion."

"I think so, too," Cubie said. "She's cut our abilities to communicate, or we would have been rescued by now."

Therese pressed her lips to Than's cheek, which was clammy and cool, but not deathly cold.

"Than, baby, wake up."

She kissed him on the lips, again and again and, when he didn't respond, nestled her face against his, praying to him about how much she loved him and wanted to be with him.

As Therese lay beside Than, she regretted having ever postponed their wedding, They could be united in marriage by now, a complete family. She had allowed her foolish fears of infidelity among the gods to cloud her judgment. She should have never doubted Than's love for her.

The goat that had been left behind by the two nymphs brayed a complaint. Apparently it was time for her to be milked, and her teats were full and uncomfortable. This gave Therese an idea.

"I can help you feel better," Therese said to the goat. "Come here."

The goat hesitated, but then took a few steps in Therese's direction.

"Come closer to me, and I will drink from your teats and relieve the pressure for you," Therese said gently.

The goat, apparently desperate, positioned herself over Therese and allowed Therese to drink her milk. Although it felt strange to suckle the soft fuzzy teats of the goat, the milk was warm, sweet, and delicious. Therese took some in her mouth and then pulled away to drizzle it onto Than's parched lips.

When Than didn't react, she tried once more, instructing the goat to go to Cubie and Galin and let them drink.

"Do I really have to drink from a goat?" Cubie asked. "It feels awkward, with my being a Doberman and all."

"If we help her, she might help us," Galin said.

While the others drank from the goat, Therese drizzled more of the milk across Than's lips. At first the milk dripped along the sides of his chin and there was no reaction from him, but after a few moments, just as she was about to give up, she saw his tongue move across his lips and lick up the milk. Encouraged by this, Therese allowed more of the milk to drip from her mouth into his and was relieved to see him drink. He blinked and opened his eyes.

"Than?" she asked with her face near his. "Can you hear me?"

He blinked again and groaned. *I can't move*, he replied through prayer.

She asked the she-goat to return to her so Therese could suckle more milk for Than. When her mouth was full of milk, she prayed, *Drink this.*

He swallowed the milk she passed to him. She was so happy, that as soon as her mouth was empty of milk, she pressed her lips to his.

"Oh, Than! I'm so relieved you're awake. Are you in pain?"

Just sore and immobile. How long have I been out?

I don't know. Maybe an hour or two?

"He's awake?" Cubie asked from across the cave.

"Can he speak?" Galin asked.

"He's awake but paralyzed," Therese explained. "I think the goat's milk is helping him."

Therese reached behind her shoulder with her chin and grabbed an arrow from her quiver with her teeth. Then she pierced the goat's heart, to insure the goat would remain loyal to them once she had emptied her milk.

"Can you eat away the leather on my wrists?" Therese asked the goat.

Chapter Fifteen: The Old Man of the Sea

At the same time Hip was informing his parents of Odysseus's information about Than and Therese and a plan was being hatched to save Thanatos and the others from the Malevolent, a disintegrated Hip rode beside Apollo and his sisters in Apollo's shining chariot from a chasm in the Far East. Together they soared high above the clouds and traveled beside Helios, the sun god, who flew around the earth every day in his golden cup. They did this to disguise their flight from Zeus and his spies. Because they dared not go any faster than Helios, it took twelve hours for them to reach the Ionian Sea, west of the mainland of Greece, where the Old Man of the Sea and his wife, Keto, dwelled.

Like a falling star, Hip and his fellow passengers soared from the sky toward the island of Ithaca, led by Apollo's three flaming mares, and plunged into the sea, barely missing a retinue of thunderbolts. Once underwater, they prepared to defend themselves from attacks by Poseidon and his beasts.

The fire of Apollo's horses shined brightly beneath the surface, and together with the golden chariot and the five gods, they created an underwater spotlight for miles and miles, unsettling the creatures of the sea.

"You're sure this is the way?" Hip asked Apollo.

"I know where Phorcys and Keto live," Apollo replied.

"I mean storming into the sea, bright and obvious rather than incognito."

"We can't hide from Poseidon, so we may as well be aggressive and fearsome in our approach."

That made sense to Hip, but it didn't make him feel any more confident.

Sure enough, as the chariot sped past an underwater volcano, a great beast leapt from it like black lava and hurled itself at the five gods.

"It's a giant octopus!" Meg cried.

Hip grit his teeth and conjured his weapon.

All five of them lifted their blades defensively as the beast descended. Hip prayed to the Old Man of the Sea to come to their rescue. He also reached out to Pasithea, his old fiancé, and pleaded with her to come and calm the beast. She appeared but seemed to have no effect on the sea monster's mood, so Hip sent her home.

Alecto swam from the chariot toward the beast with her sword outstretched. Her serpent uncoiled itself from her neck and opened his mouth to strike.

Go on without me, Alecto insisted. *I'll distract the beast as best I can.*

In spite of Alecto's command, Meg and Tizzie followed their sister into the manifold of enormous black tentacles swinging wildly at them. Hip made to follow them, too, but Apollo stopped him.

"Let the Furies handle it. You come with me."

Apollo steered the bright chariot past the volcano and beyond the reef to a deep abyss that was ominously devoid of sea life.

Apollo pointed. "There."

Thousands of feet below, in the profound depths of the Ionian Sea, Hip spied a castle made of rock. Unlike Poseidon's palace, which was built of transparent crystals and effervescent mother-of-pearl, the castle belonging to Phorcys and Keto was crude and rudimentary. The rock of the structure was uneven and covered with algae and barnacles. It was also much smaller than Poseidon's palace and, apparently, less guarded. Apollo pulled the chariot to a halt at the massive wooden door and waited for someone to answer.

***

As the goat attempted to chomp through the magically warded leather straps at Therese's wrists and ankles, Therese watched Than go in and out of consciousness. He lay beside her, still paralyzed and unable to speak. Occasionally he connected with her through prayer, but these communications were brief and intermittent.

Therese pressed her lips to Than's ears and told him again and again how much she loved him and how sorry she was for ever doubting his ability to remain faithful to her. She told him she wanted to marry him and to spend all eternity with him, as they had

155

planned, and she promised that as soon as they were out of this mess and things were back to normal, they would plan a wedding and make it official. Whether Than was conscious or not, she continued to speak to him tenderly, hoping to bring him back. She spoke of happier times, of trips they had taken together not long after she had first moved in with him.

She was especially fond of the time he went with her to visit Asterion and Ariadne for the first time on this very island. She had gone twice before without him and had told him about their fun games of night Frisbee. This was a game the brother and sister invented decades ago when Poseidon gifted a golden disc to Asterion. Late at night when no tourists were around, the siblings would emerge from the labyrinth beneath the palace ruins, and they would toss the Frisbee high in the night sky, often above the clouds, and race one another to retrieve it. Whoever caught the disc earned the right to throw it.

The first time they had invited Therese to play, she soon learned that being the disc thrower did not give you an advantage over the others in catching the disc. With their sharp godly skills, the gods not throwing could anticipate the direction of the disc's flight, and they often collided in their efforts to win.

The first time Than joined them in their game, he introduced a new technique in disc throwing. Since he flew all the time, and had been flying for centuries, he better understood the wind currents and could use them, along with the way he angled his release, to throw the Frisbee like a boomerang. Than could make the golden disc fly right back to him. Therese and the siblings tried and tried, but they never had the same success with the disc as the god of death.

As she recounted her memories of their games to him, she called him her "expert disc thrower," and she kissed his cheek and begged him to wake up so they might soon again play night Frisbee with Ariadne and Asterion.

***

Jen tossed and turned in her bed, unable to fall asleep, which frustrated her because she wanted to find Hip. She had so many questions and was terrified for Therese. Glancing again at the digital clock beside her bed, she saw it was already three in the morning, and she still hadn't slept a wink, yet she was so tired, and her body ached. Tears of frustration and anxiety welled in her eyes as she rolled over for the hundredth time and punched her pillow.

A creak on the floor outside her door made her stiffen and hold completely still. She held her breath as she anticipated hearing another sound. For years, that very creak had filled her with dread, because the sound almost always meant her dad was coming.

Now he was miles away in Durango at an assisted living center, so who was creeping down the hall to her room? She took another breath, grabbed her crown from the nightstand, and listened.

A soft rap came at her door. She sat up and turned on the lamp by her bed.

"Who is it?" she asked.

"Pete."

What? Why would Pete be at her door at three in the morning?

She returned her crown to the nightstand. "Come in."

He stood in the doorway in his pajamas with dark circles under his eyes.

"What's wrong?" she asked.

"I can't sleep."

"Me either."

Pete had never come to her room in the middle of the night to report that he couldn't sleep. There had been other times, not frequent, when he couldn't find a favorite CD, and he'd come in accusing her of borrowing it. Another time, he'd lost his iPod charger and he came in around midnight begging to borrow hers. But never in their eighteen years of being brother and sister had he come to her room to say he couldn't sleep.

"I'm seeing them again," he explained.

"What? Ghosts?"

He nodded.

Her mouth fell open. She wasn't exactly sure how to react to that. More than ever, she believed Pete. Her heart raced in her chest and she gnawed on her bottom lip.

Pete sat on her bean bag chair in the corner of her room and folded his arms across his chest. "This hasn't happened since I was twelve or thirteen. I had stopped believing in ghosts. Maybe I'm just sick in the head."

Jen didn't want her brother thinking there was something wrong with him. "You're not sick in the head."

"How do you know? You can't see them. Can you?"

She shook her head, debating whether she should tell him about what had happened to her. Would he believe her if she did?

"Do you see any ghosts right now?" She pulled her covers up to her neck and glanced suspiciously around the room.

Pete put his face in his hands and nodded without meeting her eyes. She wasn't sure if she wanted to ask him to tell her how many ghosts and what they were like. In fact, she was thinking maybe they should both grab Bobby and run downstairs to their mother's room.

"How many?" she asked.

"Three. They followed me from my room."

"What are they doing?"

He glanced up and looked over at the foot of her bed. "They look like they're waiting around for something."

"They're right there?" She moved her eyes to the spot he had indicated with his own.

He nodded.

"What do they look like?"

Sweat broke out on Pete's face, and he wiped it away with the back of his hand. "You wouldn't believe me if I told you."

"Try me."

Pete glanced at the foot of her bed. "They realize I see them and are taunting me. One's got snakes for hair, another is just some random dude, and the third one is—I don't know how to describe her. Half of her body and face is black and half is white, and..."

Jen jumped from her bed, grabbed Pete's arm, and pushed on him until he got up. "Let's get out of here!"

He followed her down the hall, spouting objections, and into Bobby's room.

"Don't wake him" Pete said. "Let him sleep."

"No way. Come on."

Jen shook Bobby awake.

"What's going on?" he complained. "What are you waking me up for?"

Jen looked at Pete and Pete looked at Jen. Jen didn't know what to say. Finally she lied and said, "There's a fire. Come on. We got to get Mom."

Pete stopped her and said, "What's the plan? They're just gonna follow us."

A shudder snaked down her spine. "Are they here? In Bobby's room?"

He looked past her and nodded.

Bobby grabbed a t-shirt from the floor and slipped it on. "Did you call 9-1-1?"

"Just come on," Jen said. "We gotta get Mom."

Her brothers followed her downstairs to her mother's room. Outside the closed door of the master bedroom, Pete grabbed her arm and said, "Wait. What can Mom do?"

Bobby spun around in bewilderment. "Where's the fire?"

Jen shook her head. "I don't know, Pete, but we need to stick together. Are they still with us?"

He looked past her again and nodded. "They're laughing at us." He turned to them and spoke to the air. "Get out of here! Get the hell out of here!"

Bobby struck his palm with his fist and shouted, "What the heck is going on, Pete? Is this a joke? 'Cause it's not funny."

Jen and Pete exchanged hard looks again, and then Jen said, "Listen to me, Bobby. There's no fire."

"Aw, crap!" he interrupted. "I'm going back to bed."

"Let him!" Pete said.

Just then a loud howling noise shook throughout the house.

"What the heck?" Bobby asked.

"Holy shit." Pete's eyes and mouth widened as he glanced about the room. Then panic took over. "They're everywhere! And this time, they ain't ignoring us, like this afternoon."

Pete sat on the hardwood floor and covered his head with his hands. "Make it stop! Make them go away!"

Jen's mom opened her bedroom door. "What's happening out here, kids? What's that sound?"

When the kids looked at her blankly, Mrs. Holt said, "Must be a tornado. Come get in the tub."

Not knowing what else to do, Jen and her brothers followed their mother into her room. Together, they hefted the queen-size mattress from the bed and hauled it to the master bath. They all four sat on the lip of the garden tub with their feet in the basin and the mattress like a lean-to sheltering them.

"It's gonna be alright, kiddos. You'll see," Mrs. Holt said, though she sounded to Jen as though she were trying to comfort herself as much as anyone.

The howling followed them into the bathroom, and Pete started wincing.

"Settle down, Pete," their mom intoned. "Take deep breaths."

Just as Jen took a deep breath in, she saw a long, bony hand—white as powder and covered with hairy moles—reach around the side of the mattress.

***

The Old Man of the Sea and his wife were not pleased by Hip and Apollo's arrival at their door. After leading them through a main corridor, Keto—who was an old woman from the waist up and a serpent from the waist down—slithered onto a couch of rock beside her husband. Phorcys was an old man from the waist up, but his lower half was a scaly fish. Hip hadn't seen them for many centuries, since he was just a babe, and he shuddered at the sight of them. As they sat beside one another on the rock, bubbles floating from their mouths, they waved their tales though the water, probably to maintain their balance.

Hip and Apollo were given heavy rocks in lizard-skinned bags, which they carried over their shoulders to keep from floating as they moved to their seats opposite their hosts.

"We don't want trouble," Phorcys said in a deep, gravelly voice before either Apollo or Hip had explained the reason for their visit. "The only time Olympians come to see us is when they have a beef with Poseidon."

"Would you like us to call on you more often?" Hip couldn't resist sarcasm. "You do seem happy to see us."

Not the best way to get what you want, Apollo warned him. "What Hypnos means to say," Apollo began. "Is that we don't want

162

trouble either. In fact, we are here hoping to avoid trouble. You see, Poseidon has abducted Athena."

"Why?" Keto asked.

Apollo told the sea gods what Cybele had revealed, which, Hip (internally) questioned. What if the Old Man of the Sea had greater sympathies for Zeus than for Athena, especially since Athena had once turned their beautiful daughter into the very monster Melinoe and Zeus had freed? Then again, Apollo was the god of truth and probably couldn't help himself.

"What do you want of us, specifically?" Phorcys asked.

Apollo cleared his throat of a little sea water before saying, "Hades has been an excellent steward of your children, Cerberus and the Hydra."

"Perhaps," Keto interrupted. "But Thanatos slaughtered our Ladon last year into a million pieces. And you know what Athena did to our daughter."

Hip and Apollo exchanged worried glances.

Apollo continued, "We are seeking your support in our mission to rescue Athena and to restore balance among the Olympians. No one is safe as long as the Olympians are at war with one another."

"No *Olympian* is safe, perhaps, but my wife and I would be better to remain out of this conflict," the Old Man of the Sea declared. "That is my final word. Now please leave. Immediately. Scylla will see you out."

Just then an enormous monster with six long necks and grisly heads and twelve long, dangling legs, emerged from a large corridor yelping like a dog. Apollo released a silver arrow right into one of Scylla's eyes, which bought them more time as Hip and Apollo dropped their bags of rocks and swam at their top speed out of the crude castle to the chariot. Outside of the palace, the Furies were a few yards away swimming toward them.

"Retreat!" Apollo shouted.

The god of truth whipped up the reins of his blazing chariot and picked up the Furies on his way up to the surface, with Scylla shrieking at their heels.

Once they emerged from the sea, it wasn't long before a deluge of thunderbolts poured from the clouds. Apollo maneuvered the chariot side to side, to avoid getting hit, but one struck the middle mare, and she floundered. Dragged by the two outside mares, the chariot dove into the nearest chasm into the Underworld where all five gods sighed with relief.

"Well, that was a colossal waste of time," Apollo noted.

It was at precisely that moment that Hip heard the distress prayer coming from Jen, and also the exact moment that Hades and Cybele finalized their plan for saving Thanatos and the others.

Chapter Sixteen: Rescue Missions

Out of love for Therese, the goat left behind by Ida and her sister broke through the magically warded leather straps around Therese's wrists, which enabled her to conjure her sword and cut through the leather around her ankles. After freeing herself, Therese rushed across the cave to release Cubie and Galin. Cubie licked Therese's cheek with thanks, and Galin leapt into Therese's arms with joy. Then the three of them went to Than's side.

"Oh, baby, can you hear me?" Therese asked, gently shaking him. When he didn't respond, she turned to her companions. "I suppose I'll have to carry him out."

"Wait," Cubie said. "I doubt we can fly out of this cave without notice. Don't you think we need a plan? We might *all* end up paralyzed otherwise."

Therese slumped her shoulders as she plopped onto the ground beside Than and the pool. "I swore an oath on the River Styx to tell no one. Since Odysseus once went by the name of 'No one,' I took a chance and reached out to him. I know he heard me, but I can't sense anyone outside of this cave. It's like there's a block around us. I don't know if he gave Hades and Persephone my message."

Galin leapt into her arms again and said, "You're a genius, Therese! I never would have thought of that loophole."

"Hades may be coming up with a rescue plan as we speak," Cubie added. "Good thinking, Therese!"

"Well, we can't just sit here and do nothing," Therese said. "You two stay here with Than, and I'm going to poke my head outside."

"No," Galin objected. "We should stay put and wait for help."

"I agree with Galin," Cubie said.

"I won't go far," Therese said. "I'll just take a peek."

***

"I hope you understand why I must take the precaution of keeping you here," Hades said to Cybele.

Hip studied the manly goddess, who only nodded.

Hades continued. "If you mean to double cross me, and I allow you to go on this mission, I would essentially be handing my kingdom over to Zeus on a platter."

"I understand perfectly, Lord Hades," Cybele said.

Hades crossed the room to Hip. "I will remain behind to guard the Underworld from possible attack. You must lead the others to the cave at Crete."

Hip glanced at Apollo. Why should Hip be in charge of this mission when Apollo outranked him? Especially when, unlike the others, Hip was in hundreds of thousands of places at once?

As if he had read Hip's mind, Hades placed his hand on his son's shoulder and added, "Apollo will attempt to block Zeus's attacks from Mount Olympus. The Furies will aid you in the capture of the Malevolent, and Hecate and Persephone will accompany you to Crete. Are you ready, son?"

Hip looked around at the other gods and goddesses, and then returned his gaze to his father. "I'm ready."

***

Therese crept toward the opening of the cave beneath Mount Ida, the whole while wishing she could solicit the aid of Asterion and Ariadne. The palace ruins at Knossos were only a short flight to the north, and the siblings could be there to help her in no time. On the other hand, she worried she'd put them in danger. Plus, the Olympian court might hold her accountable to the oath she swore on the River Styx. Asterion and Ariadne were certainly not "No one."

The predawn sky outside the cave looked innocent enough. She shielded her eyes and took a cautious step into the dim light. So far so good. She glanced back into the cave at her two furry friends and the goat, who watched her beside Than with worried faces. She turned back to the sky to see Helios in his golden cup preparing to rise.

Then several things happened all at once. A loud clanging echoed from the mountain top and the sun seemed to explode and fall from the sky. Therese held her breath, unable to move from the spot at the cave entrance as she watched the scene unfold. Her sharp goddess eyes soon discerned the source of the loud crashing sound: nine warrior spirits dressed just like Ida's father—with helmets and chest armor from the waist up and loin cloths on their lower bodies—paraded over the mountain peak and danced in a chorus toward her as they smashed together their heavy shields. Ida's father, whom she recognized by the swarm of bees around his head, led the group. Therese feared he was on his way to finish what his two daughters had started, but before she retreated back into the cave to prepare herself for battle, she caught sight of Apollo's chariot of fire descending beside the dancing men, and at the reins was Hip!

***

Jen watched in horror as the Malevolent poked her misshapen head around the mattress and cried, "Boo!"

All four Holts screamed in terror. The mattress was pulled away, and an entourage of ghosts, all visible to Jen and apparently to the rest of her family, surrounded them. The Holts held onto one another, shouting their cries. Bobby threw bottles of shampoo and conditioner at them, but he stopped when the Malevolent emerged once again in the center of the ghoulish ring with someone they knew entwined in her leather whip.

"Daddy?" Bobby said in a voice so soft that Jen had barely heard him

"Look who I grabbed before Death could!" the Malevolent screeched.

"It's not real, Bobby!" Pete said, though the expression on his face said otherwise.

"Daddy!" Bobby said again, louder, in a voice that cracked. "What's happening?"

Jen couldn't speak as she gaped in horror.

"I-I don't know," their father's spirit replied with a look of fear on his face.

Then the Malevolent tightened the whip around his throat and shouted something in a language Jen didn't recognize. The other spirits repeated the phrase and howled even louder as Jen's father's ghostly eyes turned a demon red, his translucent teeth grew into fangs, and the nails on his hands became deadly claws.

"What are you doing to him?" Jen cried. "Stop it! Stop it!"

It was their father who replied in a voice so loud that it rose above the howling of the motley crew: "You thought you were rid of me, did you now, family of mine? Well, now you can expect a visit every night! Just like the good old days, right Jen?"

Pete wrapped a protective arm around Jen, but she felt her entire body grow numb. The room started spinning and she couldn't breathe.

"Harold!" Mrs. Holt screamed. "Harold, are you really dead? How can you do this to us?"

"He cannot help himself," the Malevolent said in her eerily cheerful voice. "Where alcohol controlled him in life, I control him in death. Hee, hee, hee!"

"You wish!" a young woman with spiky red hair shouted as she came up behind and lopped off the Malevolent's head with her sword.

Jen closed her eyes for a moment, so horrible was the sight of the severed neck looming before them. She immediately opened them again, out of fear and necessity.

Two more exotic-looking young women—one with snakes in her hair (was that Tizzie?) and another with a falcon on her shoulder (Meg?)—descended and chopped off each of the Malevolent's arms. The monster continued to shriek and howl—she wasn't dead! And her entourage of ghosts defended her against the three women as the Holts helplessly looked on, screaming at the top of their lungs, as if they were riding a runaway train.

In the middle of the chaos, a familiar and welcome sight appeared. It was Hip!

***

Therese returned to the cave to tell the others what she'd seen.

"We have to get Than up and ready to go!" she said.

The goat asked if she was coming, too, and since Therese could never abandon an innocent animal, she said the only thing she could say. "Yes."

As Therese lifted the love of her life into her arms with the help of her three animal friends, Hecate rushed inside and shouted, "Hurry! This way!"

Persephone appeared, and together, they helped Than and the goat into the blazing chariot before climbing inside themselves. The warriors continued to dance and crash their shields all around them, and Therese soon realized they were a diversion and a cover for the rescue mission.

"This will be the tricky part," Hip warned once they were all inside.

He eased the chariot up the mountain with the dancing warriors singing and banging their shields all the way to the peak.

"Apollo is trying to divert Zeus, but be prepared in case he fails," Hip warned as they left the mountain and the protection of the dancing warriors and plunged, openly visible, into the morning sky over Crete.

As they left the island, a huge wave lifted from the sea and threatened to overtake the chariot. Therese prayed to Asterion and Ariadne to help. Asterion said he would distract Poseidon as best as could, but the wave did not subside. Two giant claws reached from the water and latched onto the outside flaming mares. Hecate leapt toward the crab and chopped off one of the pincers with her sword. Persephone followed Hecate's lead and did the same on the other side. The injured mares faltered, but had enough fight in them to leap past the sea and down toward the Hydra's hill, through the sinkhole of Lerna, and into the Underworld.

Than lay unconscious as Hip pulled the chariot to a halt. Apollo arrived to work his magic on Than and the injured horses. At the same time, Cubie and Galin leapt into Hecate's arms and cried tears of joy.

Therese watched anxiously as Apollo stretched Than out on the cold hard ground and placed his hands on Than's head and heart.

Therese moved beside them, unable to prevent herself from praying to Apollo.

Please help him, Apollo. Please wake him up. Is he going to be okay? Will he be able to move again?

Apollo didn't reply as he focused on his work.

Hip knelt beside Therese and gave her a confident wink.

Than will be alright. He's in good hands.

Therese smiled gratefully at Hip.

Persephone, Hecate, and the animals circled around Than, and Therese could feel their prayers and hopes, all of them willing Than to wake up.

After several minutes, one of Than's arms lifted, and he moved his hand to his chest. Then he bent each leg, turning side to side, as if waking from a bad dream. Therese covered her mouth and held her breath.

Persephone cried, "Wake up, sweetheart!"

When Than opened his eyes and sat up, Therese fell on him and cried like a baby.

He replied with a tender kiss.

"The party's not over yet," Hip said.

***

Than felt his duties as god of the dead transfer back to him, and he disintegrated into the thousands to answer the call of the dying souls around the world. He was glad to finally have Therese back in his arms, but it seemed their reunion must be postponed.

"The Furies and I need your help with the Malevolent," Hip informed them.

"Where?" Than asked.

"The Holts' place."

Than and Therese exchanged worried looks.

"I'm already there with Father's chariot," Hip said. "Than, you can disintegrate and dispatch there immediately, but Therese, you should take Apollo's chariot, if Apollo will allow it."

"I'm glad to serve," Apollo replied.

"I can come as well," Hecate said.

"As can I," said Perephone.

Than wouldn't dare leave Therese's side, so although he dispatched and arrived on the scene before Apollo's chariot, one of him stayed behind to accompany Therese and the others across the sky to Colorado, where the sun was just beginning to rise.

As the goddess of ghosts, the Malevolent's soul was impossible to separate from her dismembered body, unlike every other deity in existence. This meant that, even in pieces, she struggled to command her army of ghouls against them. The Furies had been right to cut her up, however, because it weakened her and made her more vulnerable to capture. The team of gods needed to trap each part of Melinoe's body and haul it to the Underworld where they would place her into the custody of Hades.

Alecto was already in the process of binding the Malevolent's head with her snake up in the air when Than arrived on the scene. Meg and Tizzie each held an arm, and Hip, disintegrated into the twenties, held the torso and legs. But the army of ghosts would not let go of their mistress, and there were so many of them that the gods could not break free.

Than and the rest of the gods focused on fighting off the ghosts that feverishly clung to Melinoe's body. Hip leapt into their father's chariot with parts of the Malevolent and took the reins of Swift and Sure. Alecto managed to follow with the Malevolent's head. Tizzie and Meg joined her with the arms, and then they took off for the Underworld with Persephone at the back of the chariot, prepared to fight off any attack.

Hecate remained with Therese and a multitude of Thans to scatter the ghosts left behind. Unfortunately, the ghosts that were under the Malevolent's power were past being saved. Without their mistress, they would likely wander aimlessly about the earth. Than wished there was something he could do to give them peace, but he could think of nothing. The bind that called him to the newly dying had been severed from these souls by Melinoe, and Than had no power to guide them to Charon. Once their mistress had been gone for many minutes, the ghosts became frightened and docile, and soon they left, except for the ghost of Mr. Holt, and Than turned his attention to the shivering members of the Holt family.

Chapter Seventeen: Recovery

Therese rushed to the tub, where the Holts huddled in fear. She hated that they were dragged into her conflict with the gods and hoped they weren't irreparably harmed.

"They're gone now. It's going to be okay," she told them.

She watched the soul of Mr. Holt amble over to the kitchen. No one but Pete seemed able to see him anymore.

Hip came alongside them, too. "I could ask my old fiancé, Pasithea…"

"You have a fiancé?" Jen asked in a broken, weary voice, her eyes half-closed.

"Not anymore," Hip explained. "That was a long time ago."

Mrs. Holt closed her eyes, and her breathing became erratic. Therese realized Than's presence was killing her.

"You've got to get away from here, Than!" she cried. "And you, too, Hip. You forget you're not in mortal form, and you're both going to either put them to sleep or kill them. Now go on, so I can to get them out of this tub."

Than and Hip both gave her a frown before they left the room. When Than disappeared through the door, her heart ached. While they'd been lying together in the cave on Crete, she couldn't wait to hold him in her arms and talk to him about the rest of their lives together, but that would have to wait. She bit her lip and knelt on the bathroom floor beside the tub.

Hecate knelt on the floor beside her. "Do you want me to stay and help, or would you prefer I go as well?"

"No offense, but your presence may frighten them," Therese replied. "Why don't you all go back in Apollo's, um, vehicle together, and I'll ask Than to come get me in a little while?" God travel was out of the question during these dangerous times.

"As you wish," Hecate said, and then she left the room to join the others.

As soon as Therese was alone with the Holts, the four frightened family members became more alert. The change was immediate and dramatic.

"Therese?" Jen asked.

"Yeah, it's me. I'm right here." Therese put her hands on her friend's shaking knees. "Let's get out of this bathroom, okay guys? Mrs. Holt? You need help getting up?"

Therese helped the Holts to the living room, where everyone took a seat, still dazed and speechless. Mrs. Holt lit up a cigarette with trembling hands. Therese eyed the spirit of Mr. Holt, who no longer looked like a demon, sitting at the kitchen table. In fact, he seemed frightened and lost.

Therese needed to think of an explanation for the Holts, and it couldn't be the truth. The truth would be too much for these mortals to understand.

Pete raked a hand through his blond, tussled hair and said, "What a nightmare."

This gave Therese an idea.

"That's exactly what it was," she said. "I've heard of it happening before in families that are really close to each other. They're called shared night terrors." She was lying through the skin of her teeth. "I was, I was visiting my aunt and uncle and wanted to come by this morning to see y'all and help with the horses, when I heard this screaming coming from your house. So, when you didn't answer the door, I let myself in through the back. I heard screams in the bathroom. I was going to call 9-1-1, but then I discovered all four of you walking and talking in your sleep!"

"Well, I'll be damned," Mrs. Holt said with a look of relief on her wrinkled, leathery face. "Is that what happened?" She scratched her head with the hand holding the cigarette, the flaming end precariously close to her blonde-gray hair. She chuckled. "I didn't know what the heck was going on. I thought maybe a tornado was coming, and then, next thing you know, I'm having this horrible nightmare..."

"It was horrible," Bobby added. "I dreamed that Daddy..." Bobby stopped abruptly.

Pete stood up. "Mama. Can you call the center and check on him?"

Therese noticed Pete watching his father's spirit, and her heart ached for him. And as much as Jen feared her father and hated him for what he'd done to her all these years, Therese knew Jen also loved him and would be upset, along with the rest of her family, over his death. Therese thought of her own parents perched in the trees behind their log cabin half a mile up the road. She reached out to them with a prayer.

177

***

Than sat in the ring of gods in his father's room thinking of nothing but Therese. It wasn't that he didn't want to rescue Athena or resolve the conflict that had erupted between his father and his uncles, but a heart—even the heart of a god—could only take so much. When Therese prayed that she was ready to be picked up from the San Juan Mountains of Colorado, he only too happily disintegrated and drove his father's chariot to meet her.

Helios rested at high noon above the clouds over Therese's Colorado home. Than kept the chariot low, near the treetops, so as to be as inconspicuous to Zeus and his spies as possible. With Melinoe captured and Cybele working with Hades, who knew what Zeus's next move would be?

He found Therese a mile up the mountain from her house. She, like he and the chariot, were in invisibility mode, but like any other god, he could see her, and he could see she was crying. The cardinals that were her parents were perched on each of her shoulders, consoling her as best they could. After he brought Swift and Sure to a halt in a clearing a few yards away, her parents flew to a branch above them, and he helped Therese into the chariot and into his arms.

He held her for several risky minutes before they sat behind the reins and he commanded Swift and Sure to take them home.

"Mr. Holt's funeral is Friday," she said. "I'm going to go. I have to. Jen's my best friend."

"I know."

"So even if this war between your dad and his brothers can't wait, I'm going to the funeral, understand?"

She had a fierce look on her tear-stained face.

"I do."

From the corner of his eye, he saw her face soften as she wrapped her arms around his waist. Then she buried her face against him, and he never wanted the moment to end.

He was grateful for the lack of thunderbolts and giant waves and sea monsters as he directed Swift and Sure through a chasm and back home again. He parked the chariot, and together, they unbridled the horses, spoke a few minutes with Stormy as they stroked his flanks, and then headed back to Than's rooms, where Clifford and Jewels were waiting. After spending some time with the animals, Than led Therese across the chamber and into the bedroom, so the two of them could finally have some privacy.

As soon as they had walked through the door, Than closed it, pressed Therese against it, and took the kiss he'd been hungry for. Six months of desire was expressed in that kiss, and he was pleased when her hands gripped his hair and she kissed him back.

"Did you mean what you said?" He had to know. As much as he didn't want to stop the kissing with speech, he had to know if she had meant it. "What you said in the cave? I couldn't always tell what was dream and what wasn't."

"I meant it. I want to be with you forever as your wife."

Her hands moved across his shoulders and chest, and he gasped with pleasure as she returned her mouth to his.

***

179

Tears of joy escaped Therese's eyes as she kissed the one she loved, and he kissed her back. That dreadful day when he'd pulled away from her and had said she didn't have to show gratitude could be erased by these magnificent kisses, more passionate than they'd ever been. His lips swept across her jaw toward the side of her head, where he nibbled on her ear and then gently blew his warm breath against it. Chills rushed down her spine and a smile burst across her face.

It reminded her of the experiment they had done when she was learning to disintegrate. He had played with her ear like that while they were in a half a dozen other places.

"Oh, Than, that feels so nice."

He cupped her face in his hands and kissed her lips again. She couldn't stop her own hands from feeling along the muscles of his back, his arms, and his chest.

He groaned with pleasure. "Eternity won't be long enough."

Tears streamed down her face in reaction to that comment, and she kissed him back even more fervently than before. She wished they were already married. She couldn't wait to start being his wife.

As if he had read her mind, he swept her up in his arms and carried her to the bed. Her nerves tingled and jumped like jumping beans. She'd slept in the bed beside him before—though, as gods, they didn't sleep often. But this time, she sensed a hunger and an eagerness in him that made her skin ripple with expectation. Maybe they *wouldn't* wait to be married.

He gently laid her on top of the bed covers before climbing alongside her. His expression was serious and lustful when he kissed her, and the chills and shocks coursed anew throughout her body.

At that moment, the bedroom door burst open. Therese and Than turned toward the intruder with surprise. It was Hermes.

"Your timing is impeccable," Than said with sarcasm.

"Don't do this, cousin," Hermes intoned with what sounded like desperation.

Than scowled and snapped, "What I do with my future wife is none of your business."

"What?" Hermes's expression changed from desperation to bewilderment. Then, as he took in the scene, he shook his head with a soft chuckle. "I'm not talking about this." He swept one hand around the room. "I'm talking about what you all are deciding back in your father's chambers. I didn't dare confront you there with the others present."

Therese studied Than with narrowed eyes. "What are you all deciding? What's going on?"

Than sucked in his lips and was silent.

Hermes said, "Hades is planning to wage an all-out war on Mount Olympus."

Chapter Eighteen: A Message from Hermes

"How do you know this, Hermes?" Than asked, dreading the answer. "Have you been spying for Zeus?" He used a protective arm to move Therese behind him where they sat up in the bed.

"You don't need to fear me," Hermes said, uneasily. "I'm not going to attack you."

"Answer my question."

Hermes crossed the room and sat down on one of the golden chairs by the fountain. "It's not a simple answer."

Than studied his cousin. "Yes or no. It's simple enough."

"Athena threatened our king," Hermes said. "What would you do if someone threatened your father and lord?"

"Your father swallowed her mother," Than replied. "She's not threatening Zeus's life. She just wants a chance to know her mother."

"There's only one way to get Metis out," Hermes said.

"Zeus recovered once before." Than swung his legs from the bed and put both feet on the floor so that he sat square to Hermes.

"Times were different then."

Than stood up, anger coursing through him. "Your father is the one who attacked us, Hermes. Have you forgotten? Do you know what we've been through these past weeks? I almost lost Therese to the Malevolent!"

Hermes crossed one leg over the other and examined his fingernails as though he hadn't registered Than's words. Was he not taking Than seriously?

Hermes said, "That was an accident. Zeus expected everyone to god travel out."

"I had to save my animals," Therese said from behind Than. "I couldn't just leave them here to die."

"They would have revived," Hermes said. "All of your animals are immortal, are they not?"

"With the Malevolent about," Than interjected, "there was no guarantee."

"We sent Ares and Aphrodite to help rebind the souls," Hermes said. "The souls were never meant to be in any real danger."

"What?" Therese exclaimed. "Aphrodite..."

"Are you saying Aphrodite and Ares were in league against us as well?" Than asked.

"No," Hermes replied. "They had no knowledge then. Everything got out of hand. If Cybele hadn't betrayed Zeus, we'd all be at peace by now."

"That's doubtful," Than said.

Hermes softened his voice. "Look, this was supposed to be a quick and easy fix to a nagging problem. Zeus was going to get Athena turned to stone, anoint her with the forgetting potion from Cybele, and then turn her back to normal. The potion was designed to make Athena forget everything that had happened before her birth, leaving her with no knowledge of her mother. Nobody was meant to get hurt. My father knew Hades could restore his kingdom."

"And what about the promise he made to Melinoe?" Therese asked. "She was promised to rule the Underworld."

"Zeus never swore on the River Styx. She was to be the one casualty in all of this."

"What do you mean by 'casualty'?" Than asked.

"Zeus was going to frame the Malevolent for the attack on Hades and condemn her to Tartarus," Hermes said.

Than turned and met Therese's eyes. He knew exactly what she was thinking. Poor Melinoe. And Than had to agree. Zeus had been willing to sacrifice the quality of life of one of his daughters to get another daughter off his back. One daughter might be a tormentor of mortals and the other a vessel of wisdom and peace, but the first might have been different had she not been injured in the womb and misused by her own father.

When Than turned back to face Hermes, Hermes said, "So you see, this talk of war is unnecessary. Tell your father to withdraw your plans to rescue Athena and let Zeus deal with her. He promises to make things up to you and to Hades and to everyone who dwells here. And he will find a way to reconcile with Athena as well. Turn over Cybele, condemn the Malevolent to Tartarus, and abandon your rescue mission, and peace shall be restored."

Than was speechless. Anger simmered within him, but he had no words to describe how he felt.

Hermes said, "Please deliver that message to your father," and then he left.

Jen was surprised that afternoon when, after lunch, as she and her family entered the barn to do the chores they'd missed that morning, Hip was already there, brushing Hershey.

"There you are," he said. "I wondered where you were."

Jen arched a brow. So this was his plan? To pretend nothing had happened?

"We had a bizarre night," Pete explained.

"You wouldn't believe it if we tried to describe it," Bobby added. "We think it happened on account of our father passing away during the night. Maybe somehow we all felt it, and it gave us this super crazy nightmare."

"I'm sorry for your loss," Hip said. "I can finish up here, if you all want to take a day's rest."

Jen blinked back tears. She wasn't sure why his kindness made her feel more vulnerable.

"Working with the horses helps us," Mrs. Holt said. "But thank you kindly for your offer."

"It's therapeutic," Jen added, taking her brush to Satellite.

"As a matter of fact, Hip," Mrs. Holt said, "I hate to say it, but now that the trail rides are over, and I have a funeral to pay for, I can't afford to keep you on."

"I don't need payment. When I asked if I could help, I intended to be a volunteer worker."

Jen's mouth fell open. He had never meant to get paid?

Mrs. Holt gave him a look of astonishment. "Why ever would you do that?"

"It's therapeutic," he replied with a wink at Jen.

"Mighty thanks," Mrs. Holt said, looking from Jen to Hip with understanding. "We can always use an extra hand for however long you're in town."

Jen felt the heat rush to her face. Evidently, her mother suspected Hip was interested in Jen. Sure he liked her…but enough to volunteer on their horse ranch just to get to know her?

Despite their smiles and expression of gratitude, none of the Holts were in the mood to talk, so it was quieter than usual in the barn that afternoon. Jen stole surreptitious glances at Hip as they worked on the horses and turned them out, still unable to believe that she had attracted the attention of a god. After the last horse had been turned out, Hip came up beside her.

"Wanna walk me to the Melner Cabin? I'll give you a ride back," he said.

She shrugged, even though her heartbeat had dramatically increased. "Sure."

As they walked down the gravelly drive, Hip took her hand and held it. "I'm so sorry, Jen. For everything."

"Are you saying it wasn't all one big fat nightmare?"

He led her across the dirt road to the reservoir. The sun sat above the mountains on the other side of the lake and would be setting in another few hours. "What do you think?" he finally asked.

"Is she gonna come back? The Malevolent?"

He stopped and put his hands on her shoulders, sending waves of heat through her body. "I promise I won't let anything like that ever happen to you or to your family again. I will personally come to your house every night to make sure you all get a good night's sleep. The only way the Malevolent can torment you is if you're awake. If you're asleep, and she comes, she can't do anything to you." He cupped her face. "I promise, Jen. Do you hear me? Will you forgive me? Please say you will."

Before she could answer, he kissed her, and she closed her eyes and kissed him back.

***

His father had been summoning Hip for over an hour, but Hip did not want to leave his mortal form until he'd had a chance to pour his heart out to Jen. When she returned his kisses and wrapped her arms around his neck, he felt his body might catch fire from the physical sensations. Never in his ancient life had he ever kissed a mortal in the above world quite like that. He ached for more, but she was only eighteen, and he couldn't bear to hurt her any more than he had already.

He lifted his face from hers and waited for her to open her eyes.

"What is it?" she asked.

He traced his thumbs along her cheek bones and said, "I have to go."

"Now?"

"Hopefully, I'll be back in the morning, but I'm not sure."

"Why?" She took a step back. "Have you come to say goodbye?"

He wrapped his arms around her waist and pressed her against him. "No. My father needs me. Look for me in your dreams tonight, and I'll return in my mortal form as soon as possible. I promise."

He kissed her again, but this time, he sensed hesitation and fear in Jen's return kisses, and he wished, for the first time in his life, that he could be a regular mortal with the responsibilities of an average man.

***

When Hermes vanished from their bedroom, Therese sat on the bed behind Than utterly bewildered by the message Hermes had just related to them. Her heart beat rapidly and she was at a loss for words. Over and over, she thought to herself, "This can't be happening." At some point, she said it out loud. "This can't be happening."

"I'm relaying the message to my father and the others now," Than said, stroking her hair. "They'll know what to do."

"Wait!" She jumped from the bed. "Don't leave me out of this. I want to be a part of the decision. I'm a god, too, you know."

"Don't god travel," Than warned.

"I know, that, Than," she said with a huff. "You don't have to tell me."

She scrambled through the rooms and down the corridor with Than on her heels.

"You don't have to follow me, you know," she shouted without looking back. "You're already there, for god's sake."

"Are you angry with me?"

"No, but sometimes I feel you don't have much faith in my knowledge and abilities." She hastened around the corner near the Lethe.

"You've only been a god for two years. I've been one for centuries. I'm trying to help."

"Don't I get a vote in this decision?" she asked, slowing for a tight squeeze where the corridor narrowed. "Your father said he was democratic in his rule down here. Doesn't my voice count?"

She felt him at her elbows. "Of course, but you couldn't be in two places at once, and I, I…"

The corridor widened again, but as she started to run, Than grabbed her arm and brought her to a halt.

"Thanatos!" she cried in frustration. "Come on."

He pulled her into his arms and pressed her against the stone wall, reminding her of the way he had pinned her against the wooden door of his chambers not more than a half hour ago—except this time, they were panting from their run, and they both glistened with sweat.

"I'm sorry, Therese," he said with his lips close to hers. "I didn't mean to leave you out of any important decision-making among the gods. And just now, I alerted the others that you are on your way. I've made it clear that we should wait for you before any further discussion."

"And are they waiting?" she asked, unable to believe Hades would wait for anyone, not to mention her.

"As a matter of fact, they are. Hades thought it might be a good time to feed everyone. They haven't eaten in almost a week."

"Oh." She lifted her brows and then sighed, her breathing gradually returning to normal. "Thank you."

"So you see, I didn't take you to my rooms because I wanted to exclude you," Than said, pressing his body up against hers. "I took you there, because I wanted to do this."

He covered her mouth with his, and she smiled against his lips. He smiled, too, and met her eyes with a wink.

"I'm sorry I got so frustrated," she whispered.

"Ssh. It's okay." He moved his big hands from her shoulders down the length of her arms and squeezed her hands. "You were right. You should be there. I, um, got distracted." His face broke into another grin.

Chapter Nineteen: The Underworld Council

Therese slipped inside the meeting already in progress among the other gods, though at the moment they ate ambrosia and drank wine and spoke of trivial matters around a table that had been placed in the center of their ring. Thanatos had escorted her through his parent's foyer and into the sitting room, but then integrated into the place where he had already been sitting beside Hypnos. Than pulled a chair from the back of the room and brought it beside his own for Therese. She gave him a grateful smile and joined the party.

In addition to Thanatos and Hypnos and their sisters—the Furies—and their mother and father were Hecate and Apollo. Cybele was no longer among them, and Therese wondered why.

"Welcome, Therese," Hades said as she took her seat.

"Thank you, Lord Hades," she said. Her earlier feelings of outrage at having been excluded had dissipated into humility. No one had set out to exclude her, so there was no reason to complain.

Persephone scooped ambrosia into a bowl and passed it around the table to Therese. Hecate passed her a cup.

"Where's Cybele?" Therese asked, no longer able to control her curiosity.

"She is supping in another room with Lethe, Laodice, and Charon," Hades explained. "I asked her to leave us while we discuss how to respond to the message Hermes delivered to you and Thanatos."

"Please don't tell me we're considering handing her over to Zeus," Therese said, looking around at the other gods.

"It's wise to consider all of our options," Apollo put in. "But no decision has yet been made."

Where's Artemis? Therese prayed to Apollo, not wanting to interrupt the meeting with more questions.

Apollo replied out loud. "Artemis and Hephaestus have both proclaimed their loyalty to us, but they have not made that known to Zeus and are currently trapped on Mount Olympus."

"Zeus is paranoid, as he should be," Meg said.

"We've been discussing ways to help them to defect," Alecto said.

"But Zeus has spies everywhere," Tizzie added.

"Including our dear cousin Hermes," Hypnos said bitterly.

"Demeter could be an asset to us if…" Apollo started, but then stopped.

"If what?" Therese asked.

Persephone gave her a sad smile. "Demeter is useless during this time of the year. She shuts herself up in her winter cabin and has nothing to do with anyone."

That didn't seem healthy to Therese. Therese missed her parents, but didn't feel the need to be in their company twenty-four-seven.

"What about Aphrodite?" Therese asked. "She's always been so nice to Than and me. She's not against us in this, is she?"

"I'm afraid so," Persephone said. "She sympathizes with our cause but doesn't want to go against Zeus."

"She's not cut out for war," Hades said. "I expected her to take the easy road. She won't be an important player in this, but will remain in her comfortable rooms where she won't upset her daddy."

"I wouldn't underestimate her, Lord Hades," Hecate said. "She made much mischief for the Achaeans during the Trojan War."

"We would be wise not to discount her potential contribution," Than agreed.

"Perhaps," Hades conceded, "but she would have been no real asset to us with Ares sitting firmly in the other camp. I wouldn't have trusted her."

Therese felt her face flush at Hades's lack of confidence in Aphrodite, and her stomach churned with conflicted feelings. Therese did not wish to go against the goddess of love.

"My brother Poseidon shares Aphrodite's sentiment," Hades continued. "He would rather wrong Athena than stand up to Zeus, and for good reason."

"Justice isn't one of them," Thanatos said.

Hades looked upon his son and gave him a warm nod. "Indeed. Justice is rarely anyone's reason for doing anything."

"That's not true of you, though, Father," Thanatos said. "Which is why we should not turn Cybele over to Zeus."

Therese's heart burned with love for Than.

"Life isn't fair or just," Hades said.

"But death is." Therese said as heat flooded her cheeks. She glanced at Than, hoping for encouragement. She was a god, just like they were, but she felt less worthy and less important since she'd been among them for such a short time.

Than gave her a somber smile and squeezed her hand beneath the table.

"Are you two young love birds so eager for blood?" Hades said in words that weren't angry, but that conveyed a challenge. He crossed his arms in front of him and picked at his beard. "If we refuse Zeus's request sent to us through Hermes, we will all suffer. Zeus is the strongest god among us, and without the help of Poseidon, we have little hope of winning. In the end, he will likely have what he wants. Why not forego all the battle and bloodshed and the resulting enmity if the outcome is inevitable?"

"But is the outcome inevitable?" Hypnos asked.

Therese had the same question on the tip of her tongue, but Hip had beaten her to it.

"Great. Another optimist," Hades said—again, not with anger. "You must know I want nothing more than to defend Cybele, and even Melinoe, for that matter, but I have to think of this entire kingdom."

Meg stood up and pounded her fists against the table, causing her falcon to flutter unsteadily on her shoulder before finding its place again. "Melinoe, Father?" Blood began to seep from her right eye. "She deserves my punishment in Tartarus."

Alecto stood beside her sister, the snake around her neck hissing. "I agree."

Tizzie now also stood. "Melinoe must not go unpunished for her crimes against humanity." A hint of blood welled in Tizzie's eyes, and her wolf got up from where he'd been sitting on the floor and began to pace uneasily.

Therese was reminded that she never wanted to be on the wrong side of Than's sisters.

"Sit down, daughters of mine. You make me proud. But listen. Does Melinoe deserve to remain in Tartarus for all eternity without the judgment of Minos, Rhadamanthys, and Aiakos?"

Persephone implored, "Consider how Zeus has mistreated her."

Although Therese resented the Malevolent for what she'd done to Jen and the Holts, she had to admit that even Melinoe did not deserve to be sent to the pits of Tartarus without the possibility of redemption.

The Furies returned to their seats, and their familiars settled down.

"Apollo, can you see how this will end?" Hecate asked.

"Too many variables cloud the future," Apollo replied. "What about you?"

Hecate shook her head.

Hades said, "We will put this to a vote, but first we should discuss it at greater length."

"Artemis and Hephaestus might have something to add," Apollo offered.

"Perhaps that's where we should focus our first efforts," Persephone said. "We need to help Artemis and Hephaestus flee Mount Olympus."

"I agree," Hades said. "So let's come up with a plan."

***

Hip was taken by surprise when his father stood from the table and walked over to him, slapping a hand on his shoulder. "You, Hypnos, the god of sleep. You recall how I said nothing in life is free?"

"Yes, sir," Hip replied, wondering where this was going.

"You asked a certain favor of me over these past weeks involving the mortal girl recently freed from the clutches of the Malevolent."

Aha. Hip had not realized the payment would come due so soon. He hadn't even had time to make the girl fall in love with him.

"I want you to wear my helm of invisibility and go to Mount Olympus," Hades said. "There, you will cast a deep sleep on all but Artemis and Hephaestus."

Hip inwardly groaned. This wasn't the first time a god had asked him to put another god to sleep so that some mischief could be made. Hera had him do it to Zeus during the Trojan War, so she could help the Achaeans fight back after being trampled down by Hector and his men. While Zeus slept, Hector was finally wounded with Poseidon's help. Hera promised Hip could choose from Aphrodite's Graces, and he had chosen Pasithea. That was back when Hip thought he wanted to marry.

Luckily, Zeus never discovered Hip's role in that loss for the Trojans.

But the time before that, Zeus had caught Hip, and if Hip hadn't flown to the arms of Night for her protection, who knows what Zeus would have done to him. Hip may have escaped Zeus's notice during the Trojan War, but to succeed with the same plan twice was pushing it, in Hip's opinion.

Of course, he could not say no. He would not say no. He wanted to help, however he could. He glanced at his brother, realizing that Than would have said yes as soon as the question had been posed. Hip wished he was more like his brother.

Before Hip could give his reply, Therese said, "But what if Zeus senses the helm? Poseidon sensed it last year when I wore it in the sea. You once said your two brothers sometimes get suspicious of you when you wear it around them."

Hip had heard this about his father's helm whenever it was worn near water, but this was the first he'd heard of Zeus sensing it in the skies. He felt adrenaline pump through his immortal body as the odds of being found out by Zeus seemed to increase.

"We need a diversion," Apollo said.

"We could pretend to be releasing Cybele to the custody of Zeus," Meg offered. "Hip wouldn't have to wear the helm. He could be one of two guards pretending to turn the manly goddess over."

"But if things go wrong and Cybele is captured," Than began, "we may never have the chance to save her."

"And I fear what Zeus will do to Cybele for deceiving him," Hecate added.

"I don't think we should risk it," Persephone agreed. "Let's think of some other diversion."

"If only we had some other reason for needing to call on one of the other Olympians," Hades said.

"Apollo could go to visit his sister," Alecto suggested. "Hypnos could wear the helm, and maybe Apollo's presence will be enough of a distraction."

"Apollo could pretend to be retrieving his lyre," Than added.

"I have it with me," Apollo said. "It's in the guest chambers Hades has provided. Also, Zeus will be suspicious of my visit to Artemis. He already questions her loyalty."

Hip realized he was imitating his father's habit of picking his beard. Hip had no beard, but nevertheless, he found himself scratching and rubbing his chin as though he had one.

"I've got it!" Therese said, sitting up straight in her chair.

Everyone turned their eyes on her.

***

Than felt his pulse quicken as Therese laid out her idea. "Aphrodite has been counseling me lately about love," she said. "I could say I need to speak to her on this matter, and that it is more important to me than the tension between the gods. Aphrodite will believe me, because she already believes love is more important than war, and the other gods will likely believe it considering all Thanatos and I have gone through to be together."

"This sounds dangerous," Persephone said.

"I could go and tell them how upset I am over this conflict," Therese continued. "I'll say it is forcing me to postpone my wedding at the very moment I realize I want it, which is not a lie. I'll beg them to please bring an end to this conflict so that Than and

I can finally be married. Then, while I'm going on about love, Hypnos can put them all to sleep."

"No, I don't like it," Than said. "It's too risky. Zeus will see right through it."

"Not without Apollo there to spot the lie," Hades said. "I like this idea."

Than looked around the table at the other gods with a feeling of dread. Everyone seemed to believe this was the best plan of action. Of course, none of them cared for Therese as deeply as he, and no one had more to lose if things went wrong.

Than pounded an angry fist against the table. "Then let me go in Hip's place. Let us switch duties, so that I can be there with Therese. I'll wear the helm. I'll cast the deep sleep over all but Artemis and Hephaestus."

"No," Hades objected. "No one knows better than Hypnos how to put people in the deep boon of sleep. I understand your desire to be near your bride, but I won't risk this mission over it."

"I promise to protect her," Hip said to Than, meeting his eyes with what Than knew was sincere love. "I will do everything in my power to bring her back safely."

Than clenched his teeth in agony. He loved Therese for her generous spirit, but just now he wished she had kept her mouth shut.

She squeezed his hand beneath the table and gave him a solemn smile. *I can do this*, she prayed to him. *Try not to worry.*

She had asked him to do the impossible.

Chapter Twenty: Mission Olympus

Therese held the reins of Swift and Sure as she sailed through the chasm and into the evening sky toward Mount Olympus. Hip was beside her, though she could not see or sense him at all in his father's helm. She wished she could sense him, though, because she felt alone and frightened and was questioning why she couldn't have let one of the more experienced gods think of a plan. What had she been thinking?

This is crazy, she thought to herself—though she didn't dare let Than know how terrified she was.

A bolt of lightning streaked across the sky, and she realized she'd forgotten the most important thing Hades had told her to do.

"Let Zeus know you're coming," Hades had said. "As soon as you leave the chasm, pray to him, so he doesn't strike you down."

Lord Zeus, Therese began.

"Compliment him," Hades had said.

The most powerful of all the gods, she added. *I really need to speak with Aphrodite concerning matters of the heart, which are the most important matters in the world to me.*

She hoped that sounded lofty and serious. When the gods spoke casually to her and to others, they sounded like regular people, but when they spoke of official business at court, it seemed to Therese they shifted into a loftier conversational style. Whether

200

they did so out of custom, out of respect, or to show off, Therese didn't know.

The sky remained quiet, and since no more lightning shot down at her, she took this as a good sign. But as she neared the gates of Mount Olympus, her hands shook with fear.

Please help me to be strong, she prayed to Hades. She usually prayed to Than, but she didn't want him to worry.

You are strong without my help, came the reply from Hades.

Therese approached the gates and said, "Spring, Summer, Winter, and Fall, please open the gates so that I, Therese, goddess of animal companions, may enter."

A loud roar carried through the air, and a tunnel of cold wind lifted. At its center was a single rain cloud. As the wind settled and the rain cloud emptied its contents, the giant wall of clouds opened, and Therese drew the chariot forward. The wall of clouds closed behind her. She passed the beautiful fountain and parked the chariot, where Cupid offered to unbridle the horses. She thanked him and strode to the palace, where she took the rainbow steps into the court. She had no idea if Hip was with her.

Zeus sat beside Hera on their double golden throne. Hera openly glared at Therese, still sore over losing her golden apples from the garden of the Hesperides. Ares sat to their left, but his expression was cool and aloof. He wasn't openly hostile; nor was he friendly. Hermes was there, after Apollo and Poseidon's empty thrones, looking somber and anxious. He usually greeted Therese with a wink, but today there was no wink for her. Beside Hermes was Hephaestus looking grave.

Therese frowned at Athena's empty place to Zeus's right and briefly met the eyes of Artemis beside it. Past the double throne belonging to Persephone and Demeter was Aphrodite and her beautiful, smiling face. Therese immediately felt better.

"May I speak with Aphrodite?" Therese asked from where she stood in the center of the room. She still had no idea whether Hip had remained behind in the chariot garage or whether he was beside her now. She tried to hide her terror. "My heart is breaking."

"You may speak to her," Zeus replied in his loud, authoritative voice, "but you must do so before us all. No privacy can be afforded to anyone during these delicate times."

She fell on her knees before Aphrodite and cried her eyes out. She allowed all her fear and anxiety and frustration to pour down her cheeks. Her body shook, and she couldn't speak for several minutes. If Hades could have seen her, he might have thought her an excellent actress, but it was no act. She was baring her heart to her favorite goddess.

"There, there," Aphrodite said, patting Therese's hair and shoulder. "Tell me what's troubling you."

Therese wiped her face with the back of her hands, cleared her throat, and, without getting up from her knees, said, "Oh, Aphrodite, I finally told Than how wrong I was to question his fidelity. I told him I love him and want to marry him and to be with him forever."

Aphrodite's face lit up. "That's wonderful news. So why are you so upset? He didn't reject you, did he?"

"No. He kissed me more passionately than he's ever kissed me, and when he lifted me in his arms, I thought I would die of love." It felt so good to get all of these feelings out. She sat back on her heels, which helped to hide her trembling legs.

Aphrodite smiled down at her, and Therese wished they were on the same side of this conflict so she wouldn't have to put their relationship in danger. She never wanted the goddess of love to be angry with her. She hoped she would always smile down on her as she was smiling at her now.

"Love is overwhelming at times," the goddess said as she stole a glance across the room at Ares.

"We agreed to plan our wedding as soon as possible," Therese continued, "but before we could tell everyone that the wedding was back on, Hermes appeared to us with Zeus's message."

Everyone looked at Zeus, and, it seemed to Therese, they all had fear in their eyes, even the king of the gods.

"Now this conflict between brothers is ruining everything!" Therese said, the sobs overcoming her. She wondered how much longer before Hypnos would lure everyone to sleep. She would soon run out of things to say. "Who knows when we'll be married the way things are going?"

Zeus spoke next. "Do you know what my brother plans to do, Therese? Will he turn over Cybele, as I asked, and put Melinoe into the pits of Tartarus? Or does he plan to go against my wishes and force my hand?"

Therese wiped her eyes again, and sat up on her knees. "Lord Zeus, I only know he is discussing his options with the other gods in his chambers. I hope he will do as you ask, so that we can put this behind us and Than and I can finally be married." She felt guilty over the lie, but she was terrified to tell him what she really thought.

"I hope so too, child," Zeus replied. "Perhaps your coming here is a good omen. If you truly wish to bring a speedy end to this conflict, you should come back here and report to me the moment Hades has made a decision, whether favorable or unfavorable, to me. Do you agree?"

Where was Hypnos? Why weren't the gods falling asleep yet? Therese didn't want to make a promise to the king of gods when she had no intentions of keeping her word.

***

After Therese had parked the chariot, Hip had followed her out to the garage only to become wary near the fountain, because he knew that every time his father had worn the helm in or near water, Poseidon had found him out. To avoid a possible snag in their plan, Hip went a different route to the palace. He first entered the back door of Hephaestus's forge and maneuvered his way through all of the machinery and metal work to the door leading into the palace.

Hip found it impossible to travel through the door. If he were to open it, he'd risk giving himself away. He cursed and traced his steps back through the machinery and metal work to the back door, all the while thinking of another way to get into the palace.

He decided to go all the way around the back side, making a circle to the front of the building on the opposite side of the façade from the forge. This was the kitchen, and sure enough, he found Hestia busy at work making up wonderful dishes for dipping into ambrosia sauce. He resisted the urge to dip his finger into the sauce pan as he made his way through the door and into the palace.

***

"I don't want to get in trouble with Than's father," Therese said to Zeus. "What if he won't allow Than to marry me? I'll be heartbroken forever." She shook with sobs at the thought of it and was relieved to see compassion rather than anger on Zeus's face.

"Dear child," he began, "I am the lord of all gods. If you do this favor for me, I will make sure that you and Thanatos have the best wedding imaginable. We will have the muses sing, and Hermes will play something lovely on his pipe, and perhaps Apollo will join him on his lyre. Hestia will make us the best banquet possible, and I will ask Hephaestus to create an arch of gold beneath which you and your groom shall exchange your nuptial vows. No god will stand in the way of your marriage."

Therese wished Zeus hadn't been willing to sacrifice Melinoe for his own sake, even though Melinoe was cruel. She also wished he weren't planning to imprison Cybele, who was only trying to stand up for Melinoe and Athena. Zeus could be so kind and agreeable. She liked so much about him. He was handsome, funny, and kind. He spoke eloquently and showed compassion. He had reigned over the gods of Mount Olympus for centuries, and everyone respected him. Why did he have to screw everything up?

Therese couldn't stop herself from asking her question, "Why can't we just go back to the way things were?"

"I wish we could. I can't tell you how hard I wish it. But Athena wants me to release her mother, and doing so will endanger me and my ability to rule. A threat to the king must be dealt with, you understand? I tried to do it in a way that would bring the least amount of harm to anyone, but Cybele deceived me. When someone deceives the king, he or she must be punished. You agree, yes?"

Therese did agree. Everything Zeus said had sounded right. She nodded.

Zeus gave her a smile. "Do you swear then, on the River Styx…"

The lord of the skies yawned. Therese looked around and saw all of the gods except Artemis and Hephaestus were falling asleep in their thrones. Finally! Her heart pounded wildly in her chest as adrenaline surged through her. This was the witching hour, the decisive moment. She and Hip would either succeed in helping the god of the forge and the goddess of the hunt defect to the Underworld, or they would all be captured and become prisoners of Mount Olympus.

***

Hip lifted the helm of invisibility and showed himself to those awake and beckoned them to follow.

They secured the horses to the chariot, creeping softly past Cupid's snoring body, and approached the gates, but the seasons

206

were also sound asleep, and the gates would not open. The gods pulled and tugged with all their strength. The gates would not budge.

Hip disintegrated into the hundreds and stationed fifty of himself on one side of the gate and fifty on the other. Then he pushed with all his might and was able to create an opening just large enough for the other gods to slip through.

Before he had gone through himself, a slight and feminine figure thrust her head into the opening and cried, "Hypnos!"

It was Pasithea.

"I left to run an errand for my lady, and when I returned, I couldn't get back inside," she explained. "What's happened? Why are the seasons snoring? Aphrodite won't answer me."

"Go in," Hip said before he himself had gone out. "I'll hold the gates open for you to pass. I'm in a hurry."

"Why? Is something wrong?" she asked as she climbed inside the gates, her face close to his.

Then she noticed there were fifty of him on one side of the gate and fifty on the other.

"Come on, Hypnos!" Hephaestus shouted.

Pasithea, frightened by the army Hip had amassed, cried out for her mistress. "Aphrodite? My lady, where are you?"

Hypnos slipped through the gate, but before he could integrate, Pasithea grabbed one of his arms and shouted, "Tell me what's going on!"

"Hephaestus and Artemis are joining forces with my father," he said.

"What?" she studied his face, to see if he was telling the truth. Her own expression was one of horror. "You plan to fight against Zeus?"

"We're leaving!" Artemis said as the chariot took off into the sky.

"It's the right thing to do," Hip said. "Now let go of my hand, and please tell no one what you saw."

"I can't betray my lady and my king," she cried.

He took her hand in both of his and beseeched her. "If you ever loved me, you'll tell no one, especially Zeus." He kissed her on her cheek and pulled his hands away.

"Zeus!" she shrieked in the loudest voice he'd ever heard her make. "Lord Zeus, wake up!"

Hip was about to integrate when a strong hand pitched him up into the air and dragged him into the palace.

***

Than was relieved when Swift and Sure brought the chariot into the garage, where he was waiting. Hephaestus took his hand, gave it a hearty squeeze, and slapped him on the back.

"You should be proud of your bride," the god of the forge said with excitement.

"She was spectacular," Artemis concurred as she climbed from the chariot.

Hip winced. "I suppose she gets all the credit."

Than embraced Therese, fighting off tears of joy. He had been worried for her safety and had been unable to do anything but stand here and wait. The dying couldn't die, that's how frightened he'd been. Now he disintegrated and continued his duties.

The last to climb from the chariot, Hip winced again.

"Are you injured?" Than asked him.

"Caught," he said, panting.

"What?" they all turned to him at once.

"Zeus grabbed me before I could integrate."

Hades appeared beside them in the caverns. "What's this I hear? Hypnos is captured?"

"Yes, Father," Hypnos said. "Help me!"

Than caught his brother as he seemed about to faint.

"What is Zeus up to?" Hades asked. "Is he torturing you?"

Than frowned as he noticed the sweat dripping from his brother's brow.

Hip replied, "He's carried me off to Mount Ida and he's chained me to the mountain top. He's commanded the vultures to eat my liver every day until you turn over Cybele."

Therese gasped in horror and met Than's terrified eyes.

"Zeus has gone mad!" Hephaestus wailed.

"He can't get away with this!" Artemis cried.

Panting and quivering, Hip leaned against Than's arms. "Help me!" Hip said as tears welled in his eyes. "The birds are coming!"

"Oh my gods!" Therese screamed as tears poured down her face.

Hip's entire body convulsed in Than's embrace, he shook his head madly from side to side, and then he drooped and lay still.

"What do we do?" Than asked desperately, as he held his poor, dear brother close to him. "How do we help him?"

Therese put her arms around his back and kissed his hair. Then, just as Hip's soul called to him, the body of his brother disappeared, for whenever one of them dies, they integrate into the one that was killed. Than dispatched to retrieve his brother's soul and to bring him to Tartarus until his body healed. To the others in the room, he said, "We can't allow this to happen again."

Therese met his eyes, and he couldn't believe what came out of her mouth. "I think I can help."

***

Zeus hurled Hip onto the floor before him in the palace at Mount Olympus, and soon there were chains wrapping themselves around his arms and legs, binding him to Zeus.

"What treachery is this?" Zeus bellowed. "Do you dare deceive me, your king?"

Hip tried to reintegrate with his free self, but a block around the palace walls prevented it.

"Was Therese in on your plan, or was she oblivious to it?" Zeus shouted.

Hip said nothing.

"And Hephaestus and Artemis?" Ares asked. "Were they captured, or did they leave willingly?"

Hip glanced over at Aphrodite. Tears streamed down her face, and her pain at having been betrayed was too much for him. He said, "Therese loves you, Aphrodite."

Hermes came up to him and said, "How could you do such a thing? How could you connive against Mount Olympus?"

Hip could not contain his anger, and his words leapt out like flames. "This is Zeus's fault!"

"How dare you!" Zeus raged.

"You should have confronted Athena and told her you would never release her mother!" Hip cried. "Instead you went behind her back with this cowardly plan that now has us all at odds with one another."

"I know my daughter," Zeus said through gritted teeth. "Confronting her would have led to war regardless. Once she has it in her mind to have something, she will not give up."

"You sold your own daughter out!" Hip spat.

"Athena will be restored to her former glory," Zeus said. "Not that you deserve an explanation!"

"I meant Melinoe!"

Zeus lifted his bushy brows, and his voice bellowed across the palace. "She torments humanity, and you defend her? You would turn away from me because I misuse the Malevolent?"

"You made it hard for us to follow you when you attacked us and then had Poseidon take Athena as his prisoner."

"Then let me make it easier to gain the loyalty of the Underworld." Zeus grabbed the iron chains in his hands and moved closer to Hip. "Come with me." He turned to his son. "You, too, Ares."

Zeus dragged Hip out of the palace to his chariot. Ares took the reins.

"Where to?" Ares asked.

"Mount Ida. The peak."

In no time, they landed, and Zeus hauled Hip to the peak and chained him to the highest rock.

Ares stood over him with a grave expression on his face. If Ares had been laughing, Hip would have felt less terrified. The fact that Ares appeared sorry for him was not a good sign.

Zeus then called for his eagle and the other condors that lived on the mountain. That's when Hip knew what the god of the skies had in mind.

"Don't do this!" Hip shouted. "You'll make war between us inevitable."

"Your father can't bear to see you suffer twice," Zeus said. "I'll have Cybele in my custody before this time tomorrow."

Hip broke into a sweat as the birds landed on him, one by one. Their claws pricked his thighs and chest, but he could barely feel them. It wasn't until Zeus gave the command and the eagle ripped its beak through Hip's side that the pain took his breath away. His eyes and mouth stretched open, but he could not speak. He watched in horror as the birds tore his flesh. The blood spurted out of his body like a fountain. Then the eagle snatched at his liver, and Hip flailed his head from side to side in a frenzy of madness until, at last, he lost consciousness and all went dark.

Chapter Twenty-One: Deliberations

That night, Jen lay in her bed, wide awake. Hip had said he'd come and protect everyone in her family by making them all fall asleep, and he'd said that as long as they weren't awake, they'd be safe from the Malevolent. But here she was, tossing and turning. Was Hip coming? Or had he forgotten his promise?

She heard the creak on the floor outside her room. This time, she knew it was Pete, and she was terrified he was seeing the ghosts again. She opened the door before he could knock.

"Do you see them?" she whispered.

He moved past her and sat on her bean bag. "No. Only Dad."

She gently closed the door, in case Bobby was sleeping. Then she sat on her bed. "You see Dad? Do you see him now?"

He shook his head. "He's in the barn. He looks lost."

"Have you tried to speak with him?" Jen asked.

"No way. Would you? It freaks me out just to see him let alone talk to him. Are you crazy?"

"I guess I'd be scared to talk to him, too." She shuddered, hoping ghosts couldn't continue to do in death what the living did in life. "Do you think once we have the funeral and bury him, his ghost will go away?"

"I hope so."

"So why are you here?" Jen didn't think he came to her room just to chat. Something was on his mind.

"You and I both know that what happened last night, or this morning, wasn't no shared dream, right?" He stared at her hard, like he was daring her to say otherwise.

"Right."

"How do we know it's not gonna happen again?" he asked.

She shrugged, weighing whether or not to tell him about the god of sleep. "I don't know."

"Maybe it's me they want," he said. "Like in that movie with Bruce Willis."

"Sixth Sense?"

"Yeah. That's the one," Pete said. "Maybe they want to talk to me, since I can see them, and they know I can see them. Maybe they want me to...I don't know...help them."

She watched a shiver creep down his spine as she bit the inside of her lip. "I don't think so," she said. "I don't think it's you."

"Maybe if I go away, they'll follow me, and leave the rest of you alone," he added.

"No, Pete." Jen threw her feet onto the floor as she moved to the edge of her bed. She leaned her elbows on her knees and met his eyes. "It ain't you. It's me. But they told me they aren't coming back."

"What do you mean it's you?" Pete asked. "What makes you think that?"

"It has to do with Hip...and even Therese."

"Why didn't you tell me?" he asked.

"I didn't think you'd believe me," she said.

"Why wouldn't I believe you after all the crap we just went through? There's nothing you can say that could ever be crazier than last night."

"Oh, yeah?" she asked, on the verge of telling him everything.

"Yeah."

***

The gods of the Underworld sat in a ring in Hades's chambers where the table had been removed to make more room. They were joined by Apollo, Artemis, and Hephaestus. Cybele was not among them, still being entertained by Lethe and Laodice.

Therese felt uneasy when Hades asked her to share her idea with everyone present. Back in the corridor, when she'd witnessed Hip suffering, the idea had come to her, but she hadn't quite worked out all the details. She was embarrassed and afraid of making a fool of herself before all these formidable gods. More importantly, Artemis intimidated her, even though they had been allies ever since Therese reunited the goddess with Callisto.

Therese swallowed hard. "If we rescue Hip, Zeus will know we've decided not to hand over Cybele."

"Handing her over is still an option, as far as I'm concerned," Hades said. "I'm not certain we have a choice. I can't leave Hypnos out on the mountain to suffer."

Persephone hadn't stopped weeping since she had received the news about Hypnos. She pulled at her hair and struck her chest and had a hard time gaining control of herself. Therese couldn't imagine the feeling of knowing your own child had been eaten to death, and there was nothing you could do about it. But to Hades's speech, Persephone managed to say, "I agree. I feel sorry for Cybele, but I want Hypnos safe at home with us."

Therese lifted her chin. "While I was in court, Zeus asked me if you had made a decision, and I told him no. I think he believes we'll do what he wants, especially now."

"With good reason," Hades said.

"So my idea is to wear the helm of Hades and go to Mount Ida and shoot my arrows into the birds at their usual feeding time, just as they look at Hip. Then the birds would love him and wouldn't want to eat out his liver."

She looked at the faces gazing back at her, waiting for someone to recognize the merit in her idea. Maybe it wasn't as good as she thought.

"Are you sure you can succeed?" Artemis asked.

"We've seen her," Tizzie said. "Therese is very good with her bow."

Therese recognized the look of jealousy come over Artemis's face, so she added, "Though not as good as you."

"But what if different birds come to feed on him the next day?" Meg asked.

"I could go each day, before feeding time, and shoot the new birds as they come," Therese replied. "And, as long as he is tied up on the mountain, maybe Zeus will believe we are still trying to decide what to do. Then we might have a better chance at saving Athena. I think our rescue mission will be a surprise, as long as Hip is tied to the mountain."

Therese was the youngest among them and the least experienced, but she believed in this idea. She hoped the other gods would take her seriously and consider what she had to say.

"Zeus will have guards stationed there," Hephaestus said. "And they will notice when the birds don't eat."

"Plus, we will need the helm as we travel to the sea," Apollo added. "Zeus has spies in the sky, and they will spot us otherwise."

Another idea came to Therese. "What if I change myself into a vulture and pierce the guards with my arrows as they look at me? Then I can get them to cooperate with me. As soon as you have Athena, I will unchain Hypnos and bring him home."

"That's too risky," Than said. "You've already done enough. Father? Tell her she's already done enough. She's barely been a god two years. Don't let her do this."

Than! Stop! Therese prayed.

What are you doing? Than asked her.

Trying to help, but you don't have faith in me, she prayed back.

Yes, I do. For god's sake, give me a break. I'm frightened of losing you. Even my father would be at risk carrying out a plan like yours.

You don't think it's a good idea. She didn't mean to pout, but he was hurting her feelings.

It's a brilliant idea. That's the problem. I fear my father will agree.

Hades picked at his beard. "Before we can consider Therese's suggestion, we must come up with a sound plan for rescuing Athena. Without that, I'm afraid we will have no choice but to hand over Cybele, for we will have no leverage whatsoever with which to bargain."

"How does having Athena give us leverage?" Hephaestus asked. "You don't plan to turn her over to Zeus, do you, Lord Hades?"

"No, of course not," Hades said. "But with her on our side, free from Poseidon's prison, we can create a veritable threat against Zeus, forcing his cooperation."

"Without Poseidon on our side," Apollo said, "I'm not sure having Athena in our possession will be enough to coerce Zeus into doing anything."

"If only Hermes and Aphrodite would join us," Than said. "They would be enough to even our two sides."

"Hermes won't go against his father and king," Artemis said.

"And Aphrodite might be persuaded," Hephaestus started, "but she alone wouldn't be enough. Plus, there's no way to communicate with her. Zeus has a block around Mount Olympus."

"But my prayer reached Zeus," Therese said.

"Yes," Hephaestus conceded. "Only he has access to the outside."

"Can't we ask Demeter to help us?" Therese asked.

Many eyes around the room turned to the floor, which made Therese feel as though she had spoken out of line. She was about to apologize when Persephone spoke.

"I won't say anything bad about my mother, but as long as I'm away from her, she feels as if I'm dead, and she falls into a deep depression. We've tried to get her out of it before, with no success."

"Why doesn't she join you here for the six months you live in the Underworld?" Therese asked. She trembled and worried she was going too far with her questions.

"She abhors this place," Hades said.

"Does anyone know why?" Therese looked around the room.

Hades waited for someone to answer as he picked at his beard.

"Because it's dreadful here." Artemis broke the silence. "It's gloomy and morose. Who wants to live around the dead? Who doesn't long to see sunshine? Now let's move on to our plan of rescue."

Therese stood up on shaking knees, unable to believe what she was doing. Why couldn't she ever keep quiet? Why was she always so bent on offering her ideas and opinions? She couldn't help herself, even when she knew it might get her into trouble. "You're wrong, Artemis."

Persephone gasped and Hephaestus's mouth hung open at Therese's blatant display of disrespect. Therese did not mean to be disrespectful, but she couldn't allow Artemis to insult her new home. Artemis narrowed her eyes at Therese, making the goddess of animal companions wish she could disappear.

"It's not gloomy and morose," Therese continued. "Beautiful things happen down here. Souls that are suffering find peace, and souls that have been cruel to others get a chance to atone for their wrong choices and move on. Plus, there are more things than the dead down here. The rats are playful and inquisitive. Cerberus is cheerful when he's been fed. Even the Hydra is sometimes playful under the right conditions. The horses are magnificent and clever.

219

And the bats are interesting to watch when they leave at night to feed. Did you know that, when they return from feeding, the mother bats can find their babies among the thousands? I think it's by their voice or maybe by their smell. Anyway, they are amazing creatures.

"And the gods who live here are also amazing. They may be intimidating, but they love one another and are loyal to one another and they take their responsibilities seriously. No one shirks here. I've found a wonderful family here, and I can't wait to be a part of it, and if you gods who live on Mount Olympus can't see the beauty and the joy and the pleasure the Underworld has to offer, well, that doesn't necessarily mean Demeter can't be persuaded to see it." She hesitated a moment as she studied all of the gods gazing back at her. Had she gone on too long? Had she been rambling? Was she making a fool of herself, as she had feared? "I just think we shouldn't abandon the idea of getting Demeter on our side, especially if there's any chance we can get Aphrodite, too." Therese sat down and averted her head as the heat rushed to her cheeks. When would she ever learn to shut up?

As tears of embarrassment pricked the backs of her eyes, she heard a prayer from Than.

You are incredible.

She met his gaze and saw the love in his face.

Hades cleared his throat. "Perhaps Therese can be the one to help Demeter see the joy in my kingdom, which so many despise."

You have won my heart, came an unexpected prayer from Hades.

She looked across the room at him and was overjoyed to find a smile for her on his lips.

***

As the gods deliberated in his father's sitting room, Than escorted his brother's soul to Tartarus to await his body's regeneration. Hip's soul would not linger there long.

"Hypnos," Than said. "Do you know who you are and what's happened?"

Hip blinked. "Remind, me bro'."

"At least you know me." Than embraced his brother.

"You're unforgettable," Hip said, his ethereal hand patting Than on the back. "So serious and solemn. But why am I here, away from my body, and not in the Dreamworld, where I usually am? I miss Jen and want to kiss her as soon as possible."

Than explained what had happened.

"I remember now." Hip grimaced. "Why did you have to remind me?"

Than didn't know what to say except, "Sorry."

"Why don't you keep me here, out of my body, so I won't have to experience that abominable agony again tomorrow?"

"We'd risk losing your body to decay. Then we'd have to put you into something like a bird, like we did for Therese's parents." Than tried to be cheerful for his brother's sake. "Maybe a jackrabbit? That would suit you."

"So you *are* capable of making a joke. Good for you, bro'."

"Maybe I'll put you into a turd instead."

"Right now that sounds better than having my liver eaten out again."

A shudder crept down Than's spine. He loved his brother and couldn't bear to let him suffer. "We won't let that happen." Although Than had been against Therese's plan to pierce the hearts of the vultures, he now thought better of it. "We have a plan to protect you."

Chapter Twenty-Two: The Birds

"**I**'m going with her," Than said to his father and to the other gods seated in a ring in his father's chambers.

Therese turned to him with raised brows.

"Because I'm death, I'm everywhere," Than continued. "I travel all over the world, ushering in the souls. Zeus is used to my presence and won't suspect me, especially if he senses me lingering at Mount Ida, waiting to take the soul of my brother."

"He'll have guards," Hephaestus said.

"I'll tell them I'm there to collect my brother's soul," Than replied. "No one knows exactly how death works, except for those of us who have served in its office."

"What if the guard is Hermes?" Meg said.

"He'll know," Tizzie agreed.

"Hermes escorted the dead before you were born," Alecto pointed out.

Hades picked at his beard. "It won't be Hermes."

"Hades is right," Apollo said.

"Can you sense it?" Hecate asked.

"No," Apollo replied. "But my reason tells me that because Hermes has a special relationship with the gods of the Underworld, Zeus would not risk putting him in a role where he could be recruited by his enemy."

Apollo's reference to the relationship they all had with Hermes made Than grit his teeth. He loved his cousin and was hurt that they had fallen on opposite sides of this conflict.

"Think of it this way," Than urged. "If Therese is hurt or captured before she sends her arrows, Hip will have to go through his torment all over again. If I'm there to protect her, we have a greater chance of success. And if she fails, I'll be there to take my brother's soul as soon as possible, and maybe spare him a portion of the pain."

He wished he could take his brother before the birds descended, but he knew it to be impossible with the immortals.

"I think we should let Thanatos go," Persephone said.

"I agree," Artemis said.

"Hear, hear," others implored.

"Then it is settled," Hades said. He turned to Therese, who was quiet. "How are your prayers to Demeter?"

Than was proud of his future bride. She had not only found a useful purpose for serving humanity and the world as the goddess of animal companions, but she had also managed to become a key player among them. She'd earned their respect as much as she had earned his love.

"She hasn't responded," Therese answered. "I don't know if I'm getting through to her. I think I'll have to go to her winter cabin in person."

"Is there time for that?" Hecate asked. "I've lost track of Helios."

"There's only time if Therese isn't captured in the process," Hades replied. "If Therese is captured while on her visit to Demeter, we will have no choice but to turn over Cybele."

Apollo shook his head. "Without Demeter, we have little hope of winning this conflict."

"I'm going with her," Than said again. "For the same reasons I already mentioned. I'm out there now flying around in the hundreds of thousands, and no enemy follows me. No enemy could. They lack the power of disintegration."

"Very well," Hades consented. "Drop in on Demeter at the base of Mount Kronos, but don't stay for more than one hour. Then go on to Mount Ida and wait for the birds. Therese will wear my helm and fly beside Than, who will seem to be serving the dead. Keep in constant communication with me, and if anything goes wrong, be prepared to give up Cybele."

***

Therese held tightly to Than as they flew across the morning skies to Demeter's cabin at the base of Mount Kronos. She wore the helm of invisibility, which made it impossible for Than to feel or sense her.

Are you still with me? he asked again.

I'm here. I'm holding your hand, and now I'm kissing your cheek.

I wish I could feel that. Kiss my lips.

She leaned in and touched her lips to his, which were moist and minty. *Hmm. I liked the taste of that. Too bad you missed it.*

Don't tease me.

Therese wrapped her arms around his big shoulders and rode on his back as they descended toward the cabin. She could sense Demeter inside.

She's weeping, Therese said. *She might not like us interrupting. Let's get on with this.*

They landed a few yards from the cabin and picked their way through the woods. Therese spotted the altar where, nearly two years ago, she and Than had set themselves on fire.

She senses us, Than prayed. *She wants to know why death approaches.*

Tell her you bring a message from your mother.

Demeter opened the door, and Than entered with Therese riding on his back.

"What message does my sweet Persephone send?" Demeter asked as soon as they were inside.

"She wants you to first safeguard your house with powerful wards so no spies might overhear me," Than said.

Good idea, Therese praised, still unnoticed by the goddess.

Demeter stepped outside her home and walked all around it, waving her arms in the air and speaking the old language. Then she returned inside.

"My place has always been protected, but now it's even more so. Tell me her message."

Therese took off her helm.

Demeter put her hand to her mouth and asked, "What's this? A trick?"

"No grandmother," Than replied. "Please listen to my mother's message."

Therese went down on her knees to show she wasn't there to threaten the goddess of the harvest. Than followed her lead and knelt beside her.

"Persephone is really upset," Therese began.

"But of course she is," Demeter said. "She's stuck in the Underworld for six months away from the mother who loves her."

"It's worse than that," Therese said. "She understands a mother's pain more than ever, because her own daughter..."

"Has something happened to Meg? Tizzie? Alecto?"

"It's Melinoe," Than said.

Therese and Than then explained what Cybele had revealed.

"Poseidon has taken Athena prisoner," Therese added.

"What?" Demeter gasped.

"And Hypnos has been chained to Mount Ida. Zeus has commanded the vultures to eat out his liver," Than said. "He's already gone through the agony once."

Demeter covered her mouth and sat down at one of her kitchen chairs. "What horrible news you bring."

Therese observed the fear and worry in the older goddess's face. Demeter's depression over her daughter's absence was unhealthy, and Demeter's wisdom and power were crucial to the pantheon.

"Persephone needs her mother," Therese said gently. "She refuses to condemn her daughter to Tartarus without the hope of redemption, but she fears that without your help, the rest of us have no hope in standing up against Zeus and Poseidon."

Demeter covered her face. "I can't go to the Underworld. Everyone there hates me, and it's so gloomy and disgusting. Just the idea repulses me and gives me goose bumps. I can't stand the idea of my precious daughter dwelling there for a single day, let alone six months."

"But she needs you," Than urged.

Therese gave Demeter the same speech she had given the others in the Underworld about the beauty, pleasure, and joy she discovered while living there the past two years. Demeter listened with wide, surprised eyes.

"For example, as the goddess of the harvest, you know the importance of bats," Therese said.

Demeter nodded. "Of course. They eat many of the insects that threaten to destroy my crops."

"The Underworld has the largest bat colony in the world," Therese said. "In fact, there are many colonies throughout the kingdom. "

"You expect to woo me with bats?"

Therese racked her mind until another argument came to her. "Have you ever seen the jewel encrusted walls? Emeralds, diamonds, rubies? I've never been big on precious stones and jewelry—that's my friend Jen's department—but I have to admit that the way they sparkle in the light of the Phlegethon is absolutely breathtaking."

"Grandmother, you really ought to give the Underworld a chance," Than added.

"Diamonds and rubies are my favorite stones," Demeter said. "But I detest spiders and snakes. You'll be sure to keep them away from me, won't you?"

Therese laughed, inwardly bewildered by the fact that a powerful goddess and her best friend Jen could have so much in common. Jen hated spiders and snakes, too.

Finally Demeter consented to visit her daughter in the Underworld, so Therese gave her the helm, and Than disintegrated and flew with his grandmother away from Mount Kronos and down into the nearest chasm to deliver her to the others.

Another Than remained behind with Therese in the heavily warded cabin until he could return with the helm. While they waited, Therese snuggled against him, feeling high from her success in convincing Demeter to help.

"Have I told you how incredible you are?" Than asked as he leaned in for a kiss.

"Yes, in fact, you have," she replied before kissing him back.

He moved her hair from her shoulders and cupped his hands around her neck. She closed her eyes with pleasure and wished they could hide there in Demeter's cabin all day.

Than must have been sharing her thoughts, for, in between kisses, he said, "The birds don't come until five, when Helios begins his descent. We have hours to wait before then."

She wrapped her arms around his waist and pressed herself as close to him as she could manage. "Whatever shall we do?"

He kissed her passionately for many minutes, and just when she thought he would whisk her up and sweep her off to bed, he pounded a fist on Demeter's table, causing it to crack.

"Than?"

"What am I doing?" he asked. "My brother is chained to the highest rock on Mount Ida frightened out of his mind, and I'm making out."

Therese frowned and bit her lip. "You're right. We shouldn't be doing this. Return with the helm and take me to his side so we can comfort him while we wait."

As they neared the peak, Hip came into view. Guilt and shame flooded through Therese when she saw him lying there in the hot sun shivering. Before they landed, she noticed the two nymphs from the cave—Ida and her sister, Andrasteia, and they were complaining about the loss of their goat, wondering how they would get on without her.

Therese had an idea. *Let's pop back over to the Underworld and get their goat. It will distract them from us and the birds.*

Than turned around and dipped into the nearest chasm, and they raced through the corridors to his rooms in search of the goat. Therese showed herself to the animal, which bleated with pleasure, since the arrow still made the goat love the goddess. With one arm, Therese held the goat against her, so it was protected by the helm, and with the other, Therese held onto Than's waist and lay against his back as he returned them to Mount Ida.

The nymphs were pleased when their goat ambled up the peak as though it had been lost.

"There you are!" Ida called, full of glee. "Oh, you sweet, sweet mother of milk!"

"We missed you!" the sister sang.

While the two nymphs embraced the goat and doted over it, Than sidled up to Hip and prayed in such a way that Therese could hear. *Therese and I are here beside you. Don't let on you know. We've come to protect you.*

***

Hip took great comfort in his brother's presence, but he wasn't too pleased with his plan. He would have preferred rescue to being used as a diversion.

Take me away from here, Hip pleaded when they'd been sitting there awhile and the hour for the birds grew near.

Sit tight, Than prayed.

Easy for you to say.

I'd switch with you if I could.

Hip knew this to be true. His brother had always been better than Hip at suffering and accepting his lot.

And I'd let you. Hip gave Than a nervous smile.

Than took his brother's hand and squeezed it. *I won't let you down.*

I have faith in you, bro'.

One of the nymphs looked up from playing with her goat and asked, "Is that Death with you, Hypnos?"

"It is," Ida said. "Isn't he a little early?"

231

"I like to be prepared," Than answered. "If you're going to criticize, why don't you take over? Come close and I'll show you what to do."

Ida stepped back with a look of repulsion. "No, thanks."

"Then let me do my job without a word from you," Than warned.

Way to go, bro'. Hip prayed. *Looks like you grew a pair.*

Than made a face at him and said out loud, "No. I took yours."

"What?" Andrasteia asked.

Just then the goat took off between the nymph's legs and ran down the mountainside.

"Hold on, there, she-goat!" Ida said, scrambling to her feet.

Andrasteia, who'd been already standing, was fast on the goat's heels.

"Catch her, Andy!" Ida called as she hastened after her sister.

How lucky for us, Hip prayed.

Not luck. That was Therese's doing.

I figured as much. Thanks, sis.

I got you're back, Hip, came her reply.

Then the first bird arrived and landed on Hip's thigh. Zeus's eagle.

Dear god, help me, Hip prayed to all who would listen. His entire body shivered as he anticipated the horrific pain from yesterday.

***

As the birds came to the peak of Mount Ida to serve Lord Zeus, Therese shot them, one by one, with her arrows. They settled on top of Hip, but they didn't peck or scrape at him with their beaks.

Hip had broken out in a sweat and was trembling.

Are you sure this will work? he asked her for the twentieth time.

Yes. Have faith in me.

Just then, the two nymphs returned to the peak of the mountain, out of breath and red-faced, carrying the goat between them.

"Why are they just sitting there?" Andrasteia asked her sister of the birds. "Why aren't they eating him?"

Ida shrugged. "Maybe they're still full from yesterday."

Andrasteia laughed.

Therese sent a message to the goat, asking her to kick the cruel nymph. The goat complied.

"Ow!" Andrasteia cried, dropping her half of the goat.

It tried to wriggle free from the other nymph.

Bite her, Therese suggested.

Again, the goat obeyed.

"What is wrong with you, you old ninny?" Ida shouted as the goat scrambled free from her grasp.

Startled by the loud activity, two of the seven birds on top of Hip flew away.

"Now look what you've done!" Andrasteia shouted at her goat.

Therese let an arrow fly into each of the nymph's hearts, and soon they were coddling the she-goat again and no longer paying any heed to the quiet birds perched on the god of sleep.

Chapter Twenty-Three: Athena and Earth Shaker

While Than sat on the hard ground comforting his brother on the peak of Mount Ida, astounded by the abilities of his future bride, he was also on a scouting mission in the deep Aegean Sea. He swam alone, since he was death, and since no one would suspect him. Of all the gods, he was everywhere all the time, collecting souls from both land and sea. In fact, a few miles away, he was just now escorting a drowned man from the cracked helm of a ship up into the heavens and then down into the nearest chasm leading to the gates of the Underworld.

He pulled through the water with his arms and kicked his legs, speeding through the sea as fast as any dolphin. The sea creatures fled from his path, for like most humans, they sensed death, and they feared him. As he neared Poseidon's castle, however, an army of sharks blocked his path. Than stopped and hung motionless in the water, using his keen godly senses to observe his surroundings. The sharks maintained their position. None broke rank but glared at Than with their slit eyes and bared teeth. Thanatos reached out to Athena but could not make contact with her.

He swam along the line of the sharks, back and forth, distracting them as he disintegrated and dispatched several miles on the other side of their line. He was met by a wall of jellyfish, and they stung his flesh as he swatted them and floundered past them toward Poseidon's castle.

Although his skin stung and he was paralyzed for a few minutes, once he was free of their nest he soon recovered from the jellyfish and swam on, more cautiously, toward the palace, which he now saw gleaming about a mile away. Afraid of being trapped like his brother, he moved slowly, looking in all directions as he went. He used his eyes and ears, but especially his ears, since they were sharper at detecting sounds underwater than his eyes were at detecting objects.

When he was still five hundred feet out, he felt a series of strange vibrations to his left. Then he picked up on a rushing sound of movement. The sound was steady, neither growing louder nor softer. Than moved closer toward the sound and stopped short, shocked by what he saw.

Athena floated in a transparent tube that was attached to the ocean floor by a long iron chain. All along the chain, at least a thousand feet in length, swarmed sea serpents, enormous in size. They were about fifty feet long and ten feet wide. They slithered in circles around the chain, and where they reached the clear tube containing Athena, they coiled around the base, but no higher, so that the goddess of wisdom floated in full view. Than wondered why Poseidon would hold her out here five hundred feet from his palace for all to see. Why wasn't she safely hidden? It seemed to Than that Poseidon wanted to lure his enemies into some unforeseen trap, something even more threatening than the enormous serpents entwined around the chain.

Than reported everything he saw to his father through prayer as he hung there, motionless, in the sea, observing Athena. He willed the goddess to look at him, but her face was turned away. He told his father he was moving closer so that he might be seen by her, but Hades commanded him to go no further than he was.

Poor Athena. How many days had she been suspended there, alone, with no contact with the outside world? Than was tempted to disobey his father, out of compassion for the goddess, but he remained where he was because his feelings of loyalty won out over his feelings of compassion. He smiled to himself though, as it dawned on him that Therese would have likely disobeyed Hades to show herself to Athena.

Honestly, he didn't know which was better of the two, but he did know that he loved Therese because of her compassion.

As he was about to integrate and leave his position above the slithering serpents, a school of fish swam in the direction of the tube. To his horror, the fish that brushed against the tube were illuminated by a brief blaze of fire and a jolt of rapid vibrations before lying dead in the sea. Than disintegrated to take the souls of the fish, and when he neared the tube, he recognized that what he mistook for serpents were in fact giant electric eels. He now understood that the tube containing Athena was guarded by a powerful current of electricity created by the slithering eels against the metal chains. Any who dared to touch the tube would be instantly electrocuted to death.

Before he left with the souls of the fish, he looked once more at the forlorn goddess suspended ten feet away and was suddenly thrilled when she returned his gaze. Her face lit up with hope, and he, too, felt joyful that he had given it to her. He smiled and gave her a gesture he'd often see Pete Holt give to Therese. He put a thumb in the air and gave her a wink. Then he pounded his fist against his chest to express his devotion to her. He formed words with his mouth, though he knew she could not hear him, "I will save you. I will be back."

She gave him a nod of understanding. Then he left with the souls of the fish and took them directly to the Elysian Fields, where he placed them into the streams of the Lethe, for the souls of animals were not judged by Minos, Rhadamanthys, and Aiakos.

***

Hades wore his helm of invisibility and manned his chariot, and all who rode inside were hidden by the helm. Therese was surprised to be among them, with Than to her right and Alecto and Tizzie to her left, sure that she would remain on Mount Ida to protect Hip from the birds, but the lord of the Underworld, who stood between Persephone and Demeter on one side of him and the Olympian twins on the other, wanted as much power on their team as possible. Since the feeding time for the vultures on Mount Ida had passed until the next time Helios prepared to descend in his golden cup, she had been ordered to accompany the others on this mission to rescue Athena. Hades wanted to be prepared in case Zeus and the other Olympians were waiting for them.

Only Hecate had remained behind with her familiars and the lesser deities to defend the Underworld against any surprise attacks during the rescue mission—though, since he could be at many places at once, Than would be there with her. And Meg, though in Tartarus keeping watch over Melinoe, was close at hand.

Therese had learned from Hades that Hecate was a descendant of Phoebe, the moon Titan. Hecate's mother was the sister of Leto, mother to Apollo and Artemis. Powerful in her own right, even though she served Persephone, Hecate was the protector of entryways and crossroads and had special gifts for warding off intruders when she wasn't taken off guard.

Therese hoped Hecate wouldn't be forced to prove her strength tonight.

Thanatos stood in the chariot beside Therese, squeezing her hand. She worried more about him than she did Hecate, because Than would be the one exposing himself as he pretended to collect souls behind the enemy lines of sharks and jellyfish, and who knew what else.

But as they approached Poseidon's palace, she and the other gods in the chariot beside her were surprised to find nothing as Than had described. No line of sharks awaited them, no nest of jellyfish prepared to sting them, and worst of all, no tube chained to the ocean floor protected by giant electric eels held the goddess of wisdom. Poseidon's palace yawned open before them, as though they were expected guests.

Conjure swords, Hades commanded.

Apollo and I will flank the right, Artemis informed them.

We Furies have the left, Alecto said.

Therese and I will go deep, Than offered.

239

That left Hades, Persephone and Demeter to take the center. They were the first to leap from the chariot toward the palace.

With her blade held out, Therese prayed to all the gods in her company to give her strength. Her heart pounded as adrenaline coursed through her, and, along with the fear, she felt an unexpected thrill. She was a god, and she could do this.

Thanátos kissed the side of her face and prayed, *Be strong.*

At that moment, the earth shuddered and stirred the sea while making a loud beating sound. Poseidon, Earth Shaker, appeared before them in all his glory, bright as the sun, brandishing his trident. Harpoons shot out from Poseidon's trident, and one caught Therese in the thigh. Therese fought to maintain her balance as everything around her swirled and swayed, and she could no longer tell what was up and what was down. Artemis grabbed her, and the barbed hook tore the flesh from Therese's thigh as it left her to return to the trident. Her thigh gaped open, and red blood stained the sea. She cried out to Apollo, but he was above her, shooting his silver arrows toward Poseidon.

A few feet in front of her, Hades lifted his arms above his head, causing the rocks from the very depths of the sea to rise up like rockets toward Poseidon and his palace. Many of the rocks shot past Earth Shaker and did damage to his castle, but many others ricocheted off the force from the trident and flew back toward them. Persephone blocked most of these, and Demeter spun with her arms out like a bird, and created a whirlpool around them until Poseidon used his trident to still the sea. Artemis and Apollo got off several arrows, some which found their target and injured Poseidon and the entourage of sharks that had appeared beside him.

Back to the chariot, Hades commanded.

The team of gods had barely assembled behind Swift and Sure when an enormous golden net a half-mile wide dropped over the chariot. The Furies shrieked and together charged the net with their swords. More chaos ensued as miniature torpedoes were fired on them, exploding like fireworks all around them as the chariot swung this way and that by Hades's command in attempt to dodge the explosions.

Another projectile from the harpoon shot toward Therese and missed. She grabbed hold of it and wrapped it through the netting, so that, as the hook returned to the trident, the golden net was dragged with it. Therese sawed the taut line of the net with her sword, and, together, hook and sword tore the golden threads. Soon there was a hole large enough for Swift and Sure to pull the chariot through to freedom, but Therese lost her balance when her sword cut through. She fell forward, out of the chariot, which was now speeding away from her with the rest of her company.

Below her was a pod of dolphins swimming up toward the surface, and among them, she recognized Arion. She took an arrow from her quiver and sent it with her bow toward the dolphin, this time more practiced at shooting underwater. She was able to account for the current, and her arrow met its target.

"Arion, help me!" she cried.

The dolphin left his pod and swam to her side. She grabbed onto his dorsal fin and said, "Follow Hades's chariot!"

Although Swift and Sure were fast, Arion was superior to them when it came to moving through the water. Approaching the speed of light, he sailed with her up toward the back of the chariot. Than had already disintegrated and was searching the sea for her. When he saw her on Arion's back, he reached his hand toward her and hauled her into the chariot beside him.

Poseidon's laughter thundered through the sea. "What a sorry lot you all are! How easily you fell for our trick!"

To the Underworld! Hades commanded.

Zeus and the others await us there, Thanatos warned. *And they've captured Cybele.*

***

Back at the Underworld, Than and Hecate had placed powerful wards around the domain, but they were not powerful enough to keep out the lord of the gods. Zeus struck through the wards with a series of thunderbolts that rained down on them like rounds from a machine gun. Rocks the size of golf balls darted from the point of attack, spouting like a fountain onto the furniture. When the thunderbolts ceased, the room became quiet, and Than, Hecate, and the other deities stood very still. Then Zeus god-traveled directly into the midst of them, laughing as though someone had just told a good joke. Hera and Hermes followed. Ares arrived moments later, holding the arms of Cybele pinned behind her back.

As Ares arrived with his prisoner, Hermes reached across the room and grabbed Hecate by the arm. He and Hecate had been good friends for centuries and seeing them like this saddened Than on top of all the other feelings built up inside of him. But Than did not have time to ponder this long, for Zeus grabbed him by the throat. Than disintegrated into fifty and managed to pry Zeus's grip open, but the god of thunder only laughed at Than and reached for his throat with his other hand, starting the whole process over again. Just as Than wriggled free for the second time, Poseidon appeared with Athena in tow.

Than was about to ask a question of Athena when his father and the others burst into the room, his father raging mad, like a lunatic.

"How dare you!" Hades roared to his brothers.

"Calm down, Hades," Zeus commanded, releasing Thanatos. "The time for war is over. I have what I want. And so shall you. I'm releasing Athena."

Than and Therese exchanged looks of surprise.

"I explained to her why I did what I did, and she has forgiven me," Zeus said. "She agrees that the restoration of peace among us gods is paramount. So I will take as my prisoner the one who deceived me. And although it was also my wish to condemn Melinoe to Tartarus for all eternity, I will let you decide what to do with her, Hades. I have no use for her, and if you want to offer her some chance for redemption, well, that's up to you."

Than looked at the terrified face of Cybele. This wasn't fair. He wanted to shout it out loud, but knew what his father would say. He would say, "Life isn't fair."

But Death was fair, and Thanatos would not stand by and allow this. Zeus may have Cybele for now, but Than would find a way to rescue her, and he said as much through prayer to her.

Cybele briefly glanced his way, but there was no hope in her eyes.

"Once I am gone with my prisoner back to Mount Olympus, I will free Hypnos from Mount Ida," Zeus declared. "Although I am disappointed by the choices some of you made, I do understand you were motivated by your love and devotion to Athena. For that reason, I will forgive your insurrection. But know this: If anyone dares to retrieve Cybele from me, there will be no mercy."

Zeus disappeared before anyone could protest, and he was shortly followed by Hera, Hermes, and Ares, along with his prisoner, Cybele.

Chapter Twenty-Four: The Last Straw

Therese leaned against Than, her leg gaping and bleeding. Than held her up in his arms, and as soon as Zeus and his allies had gone with Cybele, Apollo was fast at Therese's side with a medicinal wrap for her wound. In no time, the flesh stopped stinging and was healed.

Therese smiled up at Apollo and said, "Thank you."

Before the god of music and medicine could make his reply, they were startled by a sudden movement in the room. It was Athena. She rushed around the dome-like chambers and marked the stone walls with her sword at the four cardinal points. Therese and the other gods were bewildered until Athena finished, returned to the center of the room, and told them her thoughts.

"I have not forgiven my father," she confessed, her gray eyes fierce.

"What do you mean to do?" Hades asked.

Athena glanced around at each person in the room, her armor gleaming in the light of the Phlegethon. "Before I say, who among you will swear an oath to keep my plan from my father? And more to the point, who among you swears to help?"

"Does your plan involve saving Cybele?" Than asked.

"Most definitely," Athena said.

"Then you have my word." Therese was the first to step forward.

"And mine," Than said, putting an arm around Therese.

Therese and Than exchanged proud smiles.

"I am at your service, Lady Athena," Hephaestus declared. He pounded his fist against his heart—the same sign Than had used to show Athena his loyalty when she was trapped in the tube before Poseidon's palace.

"Now hold on," Hades said. "I say we hear Athena's plan before we swear our allegiance to it. We can give our word not to spill the beans to anyone outside this room, but we should wait to hear the plan before we agree to act."

Therese resisted the urge to argue with her future father-in-law. She wanted to save Cybele, whatever it took.

"The newest gods are always the most eager," Hades said with a touch of reproach.

"But they are not without honor," Athena said with an approving smile.

Therese felt her cheeks get hot. She didn't want to disappoint Hades after she'd so recently won his heart, but she was committed to the side of right, and saving Cybele was definitely the right thing to do.

"I agree with Lord Hades," Artemis said. "We should hear your plan first."

"Agreed," Apollo put in. "I was willing to go against my lord Zeus to save you, dear goddess, but now that you are freed, I do not wish to further offend my lord."

"He holds an innocent, who wished to protect me," Athena objected.

"It was her choice to deceive your father," Persephone said. "We must all face the consequences of our choices."

Therese could no longer hold her tongue. "But if it hadn't been for Cybele, Melinoe might be trapped forever in Tartarus. Cybele saved your daughter and has given her a chance to redeem herself."

"If she chooses redemption," Meg said sharply. "We have no guarantee the Malevolent even cares."

"So true," Alecto snarled.

"What is your plan?" Hades asked Athena.

"Swear to keep it a secret," Athena said. "Swear on the River Styx, and I will tell you."

Everyone swore, but Demeter.

"I better not get involved," she said.

"But Mother, at least hear her out," Persephone insisted.

"I'm too overcome with sadness," she said, waving her open palms at the group. "It saddens me to see Olympians conspiring against Olympians. I'm not cut out for this. I stayed out of the Trojan War for the same reason. Athena can handle it. She stood by Odysseus all those years Poseidon went on punishing him. But it's not for me. Now, please remove your wards so I may leave before you share your plan. I swear to keep my knowledge of this meeting and your intentions to retrieve the manly goddess to myself."

With her lips pressed firmly together, Athena crossed the room and marked through one of her symbols. Demeter embraced Persephone, apologized once more, and left. Athena redrew her symbol near the one marked out and turned to face those gods remaining.

"Anyone else wish to leave?"

When no one replied, Hades said, "Let's sit, shall we?"

Everyone took a seat on the ring of chairs that remained from their earlier meetings.

As soon as they were settled, Athena looked around the room with her fierce gray eyes. "I want to capture my father."

***

When the chains around his arms and legs vanished, Hypnos jumped into the air above Mount Ida, relieved to be free and not wanting to wait for an explanation. He especially didn't want to risk getting caught again. As he turned to head home, however, the birds followed.

"Go back!" He stopped in mid-air and pointed toward the mountain. "Go home!"

The birds pleaded with him to let them follow him, saying they were ready to serve him. He wondered what his father would say if he brought seven vultures home to live with them. The birds said they would do anything he asked, and he had to admit that he kind of liked the sound of that. He also admitted it was creepy to befriend the very beasts who'd eaten his liver the previous evening, but they had only been following orders. One among them was

Zeus's eagle. Having this bird in his possession could prove dangerous.

"I promise to visit, but you can't come with me," he finally said. "Now shoo."

He turned away from them, surprised by an unexpected feeling of sadness, to leave behind the creatures desperate to keep his company. He glanced back to see them all fluttering above the mountain peak watching him go.

"I promise to return," he said again. "Now cheer up and go about your business, and maybe I'll bring you each a gift."

This made the birds happy, and so Hypnos was able to turn away feeling less guilty about leaving them.

"Bring us gifts, too, Hypnos!" Ida called from below.

"Oh, please do," Andrasteia pleaded.

"Yeah, right, ladies." He sailed away, rolling his eyes.

When he tried to enter his father's chambers to discover the reason for his release, he found himself blocked.

Father?

I can't let you in at the moment, son, but don't be alarmed. Athena is free, and Zeus has returned stability to the Olympians for the time being. Go visit the mortal girl while you still have time. I'll catch you up on the details later.

Although Hip was anxious to hear what had transpired in his absence, he was more anxious to see Jen. He god traveled to the Melner cabin to freshen up, then, whistling as he went, climbed into the red convertible Mustang and drove beneath the morning sun down the road to the Holt place.

When he entered the barn, Jen was not among the Holts tending the horses.

"Hi, Hip," Bobby said.

"Hi, Bobby," Hip replied. "Where's Jen?"

"She ain't feeling well today," Mrs. Holt said from behind the General. "I gave her the morning off."

"Is she allowed visitors?" he asked.

"I'm not sure that's a good idea," Mrs. Holt replied.

Pete lifted up his head from behind Ace. "Actually, Mama, I think it would cheer her up." Then to Hip, Pete prayed, *I know who you are. Jen told me everything.*

Hip lifted his eyebrows in surprise.

"Well," Mrs. Holt said. "I guess a short visit would be alright."

"Thanks, ma'am," Hip said. Before leaving, he stole another glance at Pete, who seemed a little fearful of him. "Thanks for putting in a good word for me, Pete."

If you can hear me, give me a sign, Pete prayed.

Hip hated it when mortals asked this of him. What kind of sign did they expect? He searched for something to say or do, but could only come up with a weak pun.

"I'll take that as a sign of approval."

Pete's eyes widened, and then, as in ninety-percent of cases, he prayed, *Just in case that was a coincidence, do something else. Say the color blue.*

Hip would play this game one more time, and then he was out of there. "So is it going to rain today, Mrs. Holt? Not a cloud in the blue sky right now."

"Usually about four o'clock, the clouds roll in," she replied.

Pete, of course, said nothing, but looked at Hip with wide, bewildered eyes.

Hip chuckled to himself and left the barn in search of Jen.

***

What did Pete want now? Jen thought when a knock came at her door.

She didn't even climb out of bed this time. "What now? I already answered a million of your questions."

The knock came again.

"Well, come on in, dummy!"

When she looked up and saw her visitor wasn't her brother Pete, but Hypnos, the god of sleep, her jaw dropped open.

"Sorry to interrupt your argument with somebody else," he said with a wink.

That cavalier attitude made her blood run cold. She sat up in the bedcovers and narrowed her eyes at him.

"What?" he asked, all innocent-like. She wanted to strangle him. "What's wrong? Aren't you glad to see me?"

"Where were you last night?" She didn't want to be this bitch she'd become, but he had let her down, and this was important. "You promised to protect us."

"But Melinoe was in Tartarus," he said, closing the door behind him. "She wasn't a threat."

"You promised to put us all in a deep sleep every night just in case," she said. She crossed her arms at her chest when she remembered she wasn't wearing a bra. "Just because you're a god, that doesn't give you the right to break your promise."

"I was tied up last night," he said.

She rolled her eyes.

"Seriously. You have no idea."

"Then inform me, why don't you? All I know is that you promised to help us sleep, and we couldn't because Pete could still see my father's ghost. That freaked me out because, well…can my dad's ghost hurt me?"

Hip shook his head. "Not of his own volition. He'd have to be controlled by Melinoe, or by some other dark deity."

"There are others? Great. I'll never sleep again."

Hip crossed the room and sat beside her on the bed. That took a lot of nerve because she was giving him her evil, pissed off, don't-touch-me glare.

"So you told Pete."

"So? It's not like he's gonna tell anyone. And don't change the subject." She noticed he smelled really good, and he looked really good, and his adorable face was smiling at her. "Are you laughing at me?"

"No. I'm just so happy to see you." He put his hand on her shoulder. "When I was chained to the top of Mount Ida and the vultures were coming for my liver…"

"Shut up!"

"Seriously. You can ask Therese."

She searched his face. Was that common for a god? To have his liver eaten by vultures? "Like, what was his name? Perseus?"

"Prometheus."

"Why? Why would you have to go through that?" She squared herself to him. "And there's not a scratch on you."

"It's a long story. Zeus was, well, listen. When the birds were descending on me, the last thing I thought of was your pretty face. And when my body was restored and it beckoned back my soul, the first thing I thought of was your pretty face. And as I lay there, all chained up, the only thing I cared about was that I would have the chance to see you again. That's why I'm smiling."

Jen didn't know what to believe. Which was more fantastical? That a god got his liver eaten out on a mountaintop by vultures? Or that a god wanted to see her, wanted to be with her? They were equally fantastic.

"Why me?" she asked. "There are tons of girls prettier than I am. Why are you glad to be with me?"

"I feel happiest when I'm with you," he said. "And I don't know why."

She had to admit that she liked being around him, too. "I guess I can't really be mad at you for breaking your promise last night if what you say is true."

"Like I said, next time you see Therese, ask her."

"When will that be?"

Hip shook his head. "Don't know. Sorry."

Jen studied his handsome face. He was so perfect. There was no way he'd stay with her long. He was too good for her. But she might as well enjoy his company for as long as his crush on her lasted. "I guess I'll have to take your word for it until then."

He gave her a smile. "I'm glad to hear that." Then he leaned in and touched his sweet lips to hers.

***

"This is crazy," Therese said when she and Than were alone in his rooms.

They weren't completely alone. Jewels was eating in her tank and Clifford was resting near the hearth, but Than and Therese were the only gods present. The last time they'd been alone was only twenty-four hours ago, when Hermes had walked in and interrupted them with his message from Zeus. But so much had happened since then that it seemed much longer than a day.

Plus, Therese felt like she and Than never had any time for each other.

They sat face to face in the two club chairs before the fireplace, where real flames from burning wood cast shadows in the room that were different from those cast by the Phlegethon, flowing beside the back wall.

"Are you afraid?" Than asked.

"Of course I'm afraid. Aren't you?" If he wasn't, he was delusional. She didn't see how this plan could end well for anyone.

He stood up from his chair and knelt on the floor in front of her, moving his body between her legs. He held her face in his hands and gazed into her eyes. The flames from the fire twinkled in those gorgeous blue eyes, and she gave a tiny gasp in response to their beauty. The closeness of his body to hers, its warmth, and its strength awakened every part of her. Where she might have been exhausted and anxious from their meeting with the other gods, she was now alert and aroused.

"We've got right on our side," he whispered. "And we have more gods."

"But Zeus and Poseidon…"

"Sshh. Listen. I'm sorry your initiation into my world couldn't have happened at a more peaceful time. But I'm also glad you're here with me, to help me through the turmoil."

"Oh, Than…"

"Sshh. Listen. If you don't want to go through with Athena's plan, just say so. There's no one here but me. Tell me how you feel."

"When I suggested the diversion be our wedding," Therese began, "I hadn't thought it through."

"We can call another meeting and suggest something else," Than said. "Artemis mentioned the Olympic games."

"But Apollo was right. Those athletes from all over the world have worked for years for their moment in the games. I'd hate to risk spoiling it for them."

Than kissed her. "You're the most selfless, thoughtful person I know."

She smiled back at him. "So when you weigh the dreams of hundreds of athletes and the risk to all those mortal lives against our small wedding party on Mount Olympus, well, it's only logical that our wedding is the right choice."

"We can still make it beautiful and wonderful," Than said gently.

"I know, but won't the anticipation of carrying out Athena's plan cast a dark cloud over it for you?" Therese asked.

"When I'm your husband, there will be no darkness ever again." He put his mouth to hers.

"But things could go terribly wrong," she murmured against his lips.

"And that will always be true," he whispered. "And equally true is the possibility that things will go terribly right."

She closed her eyes and sighed as he covered her with kisses, and for once, they spent a quiet evening together at home.

Chapter Twenty-Five: Mr. Holt's Funeral

Therese was crushed when Aphrodite refused to meet with her after Athena had been released. As she carried out her duties as goddess of animal companions over the next couple of days, she continually prayed to the goddess of love, letting her know that she had meant what she had said during her visit to Mount Olympus.

The mission wasn't meant to insult you, Aphrodite. You seemed neutral in the conflict. I would have taken you with me to the Underworld along with Artemis and Hephaestus if you had indicated a wish to help us in our cause. Please forgive me. You are still my favorite goddess.

When the day for Mr. Holt's funeral arrived, Therese was pleased to learn that Hermes had offered to take over the duties of the god of death so both Than and Hip could join Therese as mortals in the Upperworld to support the Holt family during their grief. Hermes detested doing such work, which he'd done, centuries ago, before the birth of Persephone's twin boys. This was a major sign of reconciliation on his part.

The morning of the funeral, Therese, Thanatos, and Hypnos god-traveled to the Melner cabin. From there they drove in Hip's shiny red convertible down the road to Therese's aunt and uncle's house for a short visit before the funeral.

"Terry!" Lynn cried as soon as Therese stepped through the door.

The two-year-old ran across the front room straight into Therese's arms.

"Oh, Lynn!" Therese squeezed her sister with tears in her eyes. "I've missed you so much!"

"Wanna pay wit me?"

"I do want to play with you," Therese said, pulling away from their hug to look at her sweet sister's adorable face.

Her green eyes and red hair were bright against her dark complexion, and the dimples in her cheeks reminded Therese of her own. "Do you remember Than?"

Carol and Richard joined them in the entryway and greeted the boys with hearty handshakes. Carol gave Than a hug.

Therese introduced them to Hip, whom her family had not yet met.

"It's great to meet you," Richard said. "Please come in and have a seat."

"Can I get you something to drink?" Carol asked as the visitors took the sofa with Therese in the middle. "I just made a pot of coffee."

"That sounds really good," Than said.

"I'll help you, Carol," Therese offered, getting up.

Lynn climbed on the couch between the two brothers, smiling from ear to ear. Therese glanced at her from the kitchen as she helped pour mugs of coffee. Lynn stood between the twins pointing at their faces, apparently wanting to show off her new vocabulary.

"Nose," Lynn said as she touched Hip's nose. Then she touched his eye, which he closed just as her finger stabbed into his socket. "Eye."

"That's right," Hip said, blinking.

The others laughed.

Lynn turned to Than. "Ear."

She stuck her finger in his ear, which made Therese giggle. She could tell Than was trying hard not to cringe away from her, but to take it like a good sport.

Then Lynn touched his bottom lip. "Mouf."

Therese covered her own mouth, nearly in fits.

"Mouth," Than corrected, with an emphasis on the "th." "Put your tongue between your teeth and say, "Th."

Therese giggled again at the sight of Than's demonstration.

Hip said, "C'mon, bro', she's quite young."

Thanatos repeated his lesson, so Hip joined in.

"Th," they said, spitting across the room.

"I see now," Hip said to the adults. "He just doesn't want her calling him a fan. Isn't that right, bro'?"

To everyone's surprise, Lynn said, "Mou*th*."

Therese's heart filled with joy at the sight of her future husband teaching her sister how to speak. She didn't think she could get any happier until she turned to rinse a mug at the sink and caught sight of her parents sitting on the windowsill looking in. She waved at them, and they each nodded and sang her a little tune.

Hi Mom and Dad. It's good to see you.

Hello, Therese, her mother prayed.

It's good to see you, too, her father added.

"Oh, look," Carol said. "Our red birds are back!"

"Back?" Therese asked.

"They favor this window," her aunt explained. "They visit me nearly every morning. Richard built them a nice house and hung it up in the elm—that one there, the one he saved from the Dutch elm disease. See the birdhouse hanging there on the branch?"

Therese saw the cute little white house with its little round door and its two little perches. A bird feeder hung in the adjacent branch. She turned from the window and her parents to gaze at Richard across the room sitting on a chair beside Than. Richard was engaged in conversation with the boys and hadn't heard their kitchen talk, but she was glad nonetheless to see him getting along with her immortal family.

She and Carol brought the guys each a mug of coffee, and then Therese rejoined the twins on the couch, with Lynn on her lap, to visit until it was time to head to the funeral home. Therese opted to ride in the backseat of her aunt and uncle's car so she could sit beside Lynn as they headed toward Durango. Hip and Than followed in the convertible. Through the window, Therese occasionally caught sight of two red birds flying above them.

Therese sat between Lynn and Than in the pew behind the Holt family during the service. The shoulders of the Holts quivered with their sobs, especially Bobby's. The youngest Holt was a mess, and Therese's heart ached for him.

She was surprised when Pete glanced back and prayed to her.

I know who you are, he said. *Jen told me everything.*

She gave him a nod of acknowledgement, not sure how she felt about that, and thinking, too, that there was so much Jen did not know, including the bit about Pete becoming a golden retriever last year. Therese decided that was probably information neither of the Holts needed to know.

When they had all gathered at the cemetery and the casket was committed to the ground, Therese held Jen's hand. Tears spilled down her friend's cheeks as the dirt was tossed onto the casket, and she stepped forward to toss on a yellow rose.

To Therese, Jen prayed, *I hated that man, but I also loved him.*

Therese squeezed her friend's hand and stood by her side as long as Jen needed her.

Later, at the Holt house, where visitors had brought casseroles and cakes and buckets of sweet iced tea, Therese and her family—both the mortal and the immortal—gathered among them, visiting until late in the evening. At one point, Therese stood alone on the front deck scouring the mountains on the other side of the reservoir for wildlife, like she and her dad once did. He was right above her on a branch beside her mother. Nowadays, of course, none of them needed binoculars.

See that wild horse? he asked.

Where?

To the left of the gray boulder beneath a string of Cypresses. See it?

Oh, yeah. Now I do.

As she stood there gazing over the wooden rail, she noticed Hip and Jen walk across the yard to the barn holding hands.

Although she was glad the two liked each other, she worried over how it would all end up. Hip was a god and Jen was not. Would Jen try to become a god, too, in order to be with Hip? The thought of her fragile friend undergoing challenges, like the ones Therese had endured, filled her with dread. Jen had already been through so much in her short life. But hadn't that been true of Therese when she had first met Than?

Before she could think much more about it, Pete came up and leaned on the rail beside her, frowning.

"I'm sorry for your loss," she said, putting her arm through his. "You gonna be okay?"

"Sure I am," he said. "It's you I'm worried about."

"Me? Why?" Therese noticed her parents had turned toward Pete to listen.

"Well, this would sound crazy to anyone else." He glanced around to make sure they were alone, unaware of the two birds in the branch overhead. "Hip told me I'm what is called a seer, 'cause I can see ghosts."

Therese already knew that. "What does that have to do with me?"

"Well, Hip also told me how seers can get the ghosts to tell them the future."

"He what?" She would have to give Hip a piece of her mind. Why in the world would he do such a thing?

"He said if you spill blood, the ghost will come to you and answer your questions about the future."

"That's creepy, Pete. Why would anyone do that?"

"Well, I did do it." He glanced around again. "I tried it on my father and it worked."

"Don't listen to Hip, Pete. Oh, I wish he wouldn't have told you that."

"So that's why I'm worried about you, because of something my father told me last night."

Therese glanced up at the birds, not wanting them to overhear whatever Pete had to say. "Hip was probably just joking around, Pete. Don't take him too seriously."

"Hip was telling the truth. And my father said…"

"Don't tell me. I don't want to know." She glanced up again at the two red birds. "Nothing good ever comes from knowing the future."

"But…"

"And don't tell anyone, especially Jen, because it'll just upset her to know you're talking to your dad's ghost."

"But, Therese…"

"Promise me, Pete. Swear an oath on the River Styx."

"What?" He pinched his brows together.

"I mean, just promise me that you won't tell anyone about this, and try your best to forget it yourself."

Pete sighed but said nothing.

"You promise?" She hadn't realized how fast her heart was beating. She felt the bad omen emanating from Pete. She both wanted to know it and didn't at the same time, but she especially did not want her parents to overhear it.

"I can't promise it, but maybe right now isn't the best time."

***

That night, while Therese and Than curled up beside one another on the bed in what was now their room with Clifford happily nestled between them, Therese thought again of what Pete had said to her on the deck of his house. She tried not to think of it, determined to sleep for the first time in weeks, but the bad omen prodded her awake. What could the ghost of Mr. Holt have to say about her that had worried Pete?

Therese closed her eyes and prayed to Hip to bring her a deep sleep. Her last thought before she entered the world of dreams was something Than had said to her recently. While it was true that things could go terribly wrong, it was equally true that they could go terribly right. All she could do was hope for the best. Lying there, with her head on Than's shoulder—with Clifford curled near her waist, with Jewels beside them in her tank, with Stormy not far in the stables, and, best of all, with her parents alive and accessible through prayer anytime Therese needed them—at that moment, things *were* going terribly right.

THE END

To buy the next book in the series and to learn more about Eva Pohler's books, please visit http://www.evapohler.com.

Made in the USA
Columbia, SC
17 August 2019